the
MUSICAL
ILLUSIONIST

the MUSICAL ILLUSIONIST
AND OTHER TALES

BY ALEX ROSE

HOTEL ST. GEORGE PRESS
BROOKLYN, NEW YORK

Cover Design by Predella (www.predella.net)

Published by Hotel St. George Press

ISBN 13: 978-0-9789103-1-0
Library of Congress Control Number: 2007930631

First Printing

Hotel St. George Press
Book a room
www.hotelstgeorgepress.com

For Bopa

The Library of Tangents

11
31
53
103
121
71
85

You have heard much about the Library of Tangents.

It's said, for instance, that unlike a conventional library, it is an archive not of deviations—improbable histories, oblique paths, scientific anomalies—documents whose

There are rumors of a secret subway, the means by which the Library is navigated. At old shuttle cars are set in motion. They may be boarded at any abandoned stop, the gates selves—crimson-lacquered and brass-framed, with porcelain poles and wicker seats—are entwined like roots beneath the city.

Tonight is the night: skeptical, yet understandably intrigued, you've decided to explore tracks coursed each night by wide-eyed passengers? Where do the trains go? Who conducts

Supposedly, the Library offers wondrous sights viewable through the windows of the to a slow, steady pace, the interior lamps dim and the panes become illuminated with magic which the passengers are encouraged to explore—exhibitions of various curiosities from the

With some reluctance, you leave the comfort of your home and venture out into the icy, unseen infrastructure can be found on any given street—obsolete aqueducts, rust-bitten

Coming upon an old subway entrance, you descend the darkened staircase to find convoluted train routes. The glass booth is occupied by a silent, waxy-faced attendant who perhaps he is a person at all, or an automaton, a superbly rendered machine. When you

You proceed in darkness. A gust of cool air slides over your cheeks. A distant rattle is heard

history but of possibility. You've heard it described as a vast catalogue of organized

fidelity to truth remains elusive.

midnight, when the ordinary trains stop running and all the subterranean power is cut, the

opened by guards dressed in lavender uniforms like Victorian bellhops. The cars them-

believed to be the first models set to track, and run along a network of unused tunnels lying

the Library to see if there is any credibility to the tales. Are there really miles of labyrinthine

them? Are they conducted? What treasures might be found in those deserted shafts?

shuttle cars. As each mysterious spectacle is approached, the rumors have it, the train eases

like a glass-bottom boat. Between these enchanted displays are said to lie special rooms

collection. Unlikely, perhaps, but impossible?

wind-whipped night. Now that you're looking, it's startling how many portals to the city's

fallout shelters, pneumatic pipelines, crumbling power stations.

yourself on a gas-lit platform with walls tiled in intricate, multicolored patterns and

hands you a bronze token in exchange for the entrance fee. You turn away, wondering if

turn back, however, the booth lamp has been turned off.

echoing through the passage ahead. You slip the token into the slot and pass through the turnstile.

IN THE FULLNESS OF TIME

Lost Horologies and Systems of Measure

Antonio Carrarino, *Opera astrologica perpetua ridotta secondo la nuova riforma dell'anno* (1581). Bewildering paradoxes concerning the nature of duration and infinity have haunted mankind since the very earliest cultures. Is the universe eternal and ever-flowing, as the ancients believed, or impermanent and bookended? Is time linear or cyclical and bound to repeat itself? Is it composed of discrete, atomized units, as Democritus argued, or more like the flowing and holistic "continua" proposed by Aristotle? Do the past and present actually exist or are they merely illusions cast by the brain?

TURNING BACK THE CLOCK

"What was God doing before He made heaven and earth?" St. Augustine famously wrote in his *Confessions*. If, on the one hand, He was idle, then "why did He not remain in that state forever?" But if, on the other hand, He was moved to create the world, "why did He not do so earlier?"

Augustine's peculiar question was hardly the first of its kind. Acutely aware of our own mortality, we have long been spellbound by the strange properties of time—at once rigid and elastic, boundless yet fleeting—and have sought to contain, shape or "domesticate" it, to make it our own, despite its unyielding machinery.

The Greeks did so by drawing a literal distinction between these dual features, dividing the quantitative from the qualitative. Their word *Chronos,* or "sequential time," referred to the fixed and immutable procession of days and hours to which the whole earth was bound, while *Kairos,* or "subjective time," described the river of interconnected moments that made up how time was *felt.*

Many philosophers have also acknowledged this double-pronged conception, notably Bergson, who distinguished "Mathematical Time," or clock-time, from "Pure Time," the malleable and flowing *now* that comprises conscious awareness.

But not everyone has granted these twin modes of temporality equal value.

Just as the Samurai and Shogunate of Japan rejected the musket years after it had been introduced by Dutch traders, a small city in Eastern Europe known as Havraska—since swallowed by the former Czechoslovakia—chose to dispense with the clock. Water wheels, early chronometers, pendula—all methods of timekeeping were discarded by the Havra in what remains the only known instance in world history. Even more enigmatic is the fact that 16th-century Bohemia, under Rudolph II, was heralded throughout Europe for its technological innovation, as well as its wide-spread literacy and religious tolerance. How is it that such a sophisticated people could choose to relinquish an instrument so vital to science and productivity?

Anon. Church music from the Office of Matins; one single folio in late Carolingian hand (12th century).

To answer this question, we must look at what timekeeping brought to other civilizations.

The arrangement of discrete temporal intervals or pulses was once an attribute possessed solely by music. While it is true that the ancient world had employed devices such as candles, hourglasses and primitive clepsydras, it wasn't until the Roman Empire crumbled that the West adopted a strict and standardized system of measuring time. The Church in particular, desperate to find its footing after the dizzying confusion and wanton bloodshed of the collapse, craved order and predictability.

Abbey life was soon organized by a regiment of time-specific prayers to accompany the changing light and angle of shadows. These were the seven canonical hours—sacred intervals chimed by bell-ringing servants over the course of a twenty-four hour day to signal when to eat, when to drink, when to study, when to rest, and so forth. (Our modern term, "noon," is an artifact from the midday prayer, *nona*.)

Some scholars have noted that this sudden emphasis on precise timekeeping marked the genesis of modern capitalism. Indeed, the clock was the first machine whose product was fundamentally symbolic—it "made" seconds and minutes, and people began to mark time not by events but by *the signifiers which dictated their completion*. In this sense, the collective itself became efficiently mechanomorphic, the actions of men synchronized to an unwavering beat and tempo.

The far-seeing Havra, however, made a deliberate choice to avoid this. Nature contained its own time, they argued, its own cycles, and as man was bound to the natural world, he should not seek to overpower it, but to embrace its organic phases and rhythms. To the inhabitants of this small city, the clock signified dehumanization. They believed, quite correctly, that time was inseparable from power: It was inevitable that he who held the clock demanded that tasks be completed within its increments. Therefore, instead of submitting to a dogmatic imposition of order, they rebelled against it—reversing the clock, so to speak, to a pre-*Chronos* era.

It was, however, the same stubbornness in resisting the advances in measure that led directly to their downfall. Without a calendar, much less a chronometric system, the Havra soon fell behind the rest of the developing world in matters of agriculture and industry. They failed to produce the crops sufficient to gain a return on their export; they neglected to weld the metals necessary to sustain their arsenal of muskets; they lacked the updated elixers needed to treat their ill, and ultimately, they left themselves defenseless against the exponential rate of progress enjoyed elsewhere in Europe.

By the early 17th century, the Havraska province had been eroded by surrounding Moravia, forgotten by time.

FRANCIS OF GAUL

O f the many scriptures written, copied, amended, edited and fabricated during the first two centuries after Christ, only a fraction made it into the New Testament used today. Among the missing were the Gnostic gospels, accidentally unearthed in 1945 by an Egyptian farmer, the recently discovered gospel of Judas and innumerable others deemed "heretical" by Church leaders because they conflicted with competing versions of Jesus' life and teachings.

Not all were narratives. Some of these "secret books" contained sex tips, others Cabbalistic curses or simple cooking recipes. Still others debated the mystical science of quantities—a conundrum that had raged for thousands of years.

Anon. Nero D.IV, fol. 211r, *Lindisfarne Gospels* (698 C.E.).

This quandary was rooted in the well-documented fact that neither the Egyptians, the Greeks, nor the Romans officially employed the use of the number zero. (Recall that there is no year

17

0—no one thought to count from nothing—despite the fact that there was a year 1 B.C.E. and a year 1 C.E. Because of this, as the tired conceit goes, the 2nd millennium should have been celebrated on the year 2001 rather than 2000, because at that point only 1999 years had passed since 1 C.E.) But there were far more pressing concerns in the 1st millennium.

To the philosophers of yore, zero was not at all a given. Aristotle himself deemed the concept of representing a void to be absurd, even profane. It's not unthinkable, all considered. Like infinity, zero does not correspond to anything in the perceivable world; it is, by definition, immaterial. What did it mean to quantify something that possessed no quantity?

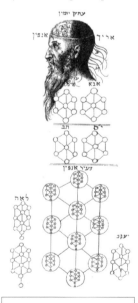

Christian Knorr von Rosenroth, *Kabbalah Denudata* (1684).

Of course, by their very nature, *all* numbers are abstractions. To impose upon naked reality an invented system of quantification that orders likely objects is a symbolic exercise, one that perturbed an esteemed Docetic theologian named Francis of Gaul.

In a long-buried epistle dating to approximately 170 C.E., Francis proclaimed that numbers themselves were sacrilegious objects. "To indulge oneself in the incorporeal realm of numbers," he wrote, "is to be seduced by idleness and distracted from the holy spirit." To Francis, the study of calculation was tantamount to a refutation of God. "There is but

18

one ordinality: that of scripture." A student of the Word must avoid the lure of "black wisdom" at all costs.

But as his letters grew more resolute and prescriptive, they also carried with them a prophetic logic. Numbers, he reasoned, were already leading down an anti-Aristotelian path. If zero was to be accepted, then infinity must be admitted as well. And once the infinite was embraced, it would necessarily open the door to what he called "impossible" numbers, such as negatives and end-lessly repeating fractions; concepts so nonsensical they threat-ened to "topple the very chassis of reality."

The theologian concluded that the only solution was to abol-ish symbolic value altogether.

Much discussion has taken place in recent years on the sub-ject of Francis' paranoia. Was he, in fact, delusional by attribut-ing demonic significance to the study of numbers, or has he been retroactively pathologized by the sweep of history? Is there any essential difference, after all, between bestowing digits with divine qualities as opposed to evil ones? Are they not equally plausible (or implausible) deductions drawn from the same bed-rock of superstitions?

In any case, the epistle, which was in circulation for at least half a century, was eventually discarded by proto-Orthodox Christians who held the reverse position: that numbers were holy. The Catholic bishop, Irenaeus, for instance, testified that there could only be four gospels, as according to the naturalists of the age there were four sacred columns sustaining the sky. Other theologians found great numerological significance to the *tripartite* God, the *seven* days of Creation, the *Four* Horsemen of the Apocalypse; many even practiced gematria, the analysis of key words in the Bible based on their alphanumeric value. Needless to say, they regarded the doctrine of Francis as a threat. The Docetic priest was summarily executed, his words, theories and divinations locked in a secret vault for nearly two millennia.

In some ways, however, Francis may have had the last laugh. Many of his prognostications proved themselves true—not only have we accepted irrational numbers such as ϕ, and "imaginary" numbers like the square root of 2, but we have allowed for a virtual *pantometry*—a system of universal quantification—to permeate the globe. Indeed, the pursuit of measure has been a relentless obsession in the Western world for at least 800 years. With the rise of calendars, currency, maps and the limitless advances in technology, man's way of thinking—and *being*—has been irreversibly transformed. Not only have we calculated the age of the universe and the distance of the farthest star, but also the murky depths of our own internal engines, our nerve cells, our genome.

To echo Francis, what use is there for the supernatural once we have calculated all that is natural?

EARLY STRANGE LOOPS

Another source of great intellectual distress in the ancient world was the question of planetary motion. The prevailing theory was that each celestial body set the next on its trajectory like a vast chain of silk reels. But the enigma arose: If Earth was the stationary center of the solar system, as it was plainly observed to be, what set the next reel into orbit?

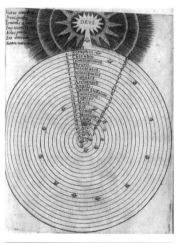

Robert Fludd, *De Tripl. Anim. in Corp. Vision* (1621). Aristotle referred to God as the "unmoved mover."

Aristotle's solution was simple: God.

It seemed reasonable at the time. Because the cosmos was contained, and each sphere rotated in fixed circles, each must be responsible for the motive power of the succeeding sphere. This system of linked propulsions, beginning with the first loop (*Lunae*) and stretching to the farthest visible stars (*Primum Mobile*), was an acceptable model so long as a third party (*Empireum*), provided the impetus.

Diophanes, a corpulent and long-bearded Ionian scholar working roughly between the 3rd and 4th centuries B.C.E., was not so quick to accept this last proposition. He believed that the cosmos was knotted—that the celestial bodies formed a closed chain of causality precluding the agency of an exterior force. The reasoning was that, just as water is evaporated by heat into vapor, condensed by clouds and cycled in the form of rain back to the Earth, so the mechanics of planets functioned according to a self-perpetuating clockwork. "God does not exert force," he bellowed to his scribes, "He merely provides the machine."

In fact, many of nature's systems, such as respiration and photosynthesis, are "shaped" as loops. Could it be, he wondered, that the universe was an elliptical cone whose mouth curved back into its base? From this perspective, the distant heavens would feed seamlessly into the Earth like a tree rooted to its own leaves. "The universe," Diophanes declared," is akin to a wagon wheel that runs not on [kinetic] power but on the force of time itself."

Of course, the underlying issue had less to do with the mystery of perpetual motion than with the elusive nature of origins, of progenation. If we are to agree that cause precedes effect, we must eventually ask, what caused the very first effect? If the Big Bang created the universe, what came before the Big Bang? This conundrum, attributed to Anaximander of Miletus, has taken on countless permutations through the ages, each essentially a twist on the chicken-and-the-egg paradox. The problem is no less preposterous when applied to space than to time. If all matter can be reduced to its constituent parts, what is the very smallest part? If the universe is infinite, how can it be expanding? Any supposition one could draw appears to result in self-contradiction.

Luckily for Aristotle, his theistic solution applied equally to all such dilemmas, and his orthodoxy carried on without serious resistance until the Renaissance. Even now, many of us are content to relinquish our curiosity by invoking a primordial agent, the particular breed of which is arbitrarily determined by our religious heritage. But unlike the ancient teachings, these traditions are rooted in sacred scripture rather than observation, undeterred by modern methods and reasoning. In yet another strange loop, history would seem to have folded in on itself, cycling back to an era of willful ignorance.

THE REUNION OF BROKEN PARTS

While the earliest paradox may have been conceived by Anaximander, the most famous belongs to Zeno of Elia. The "Paradox of Motion" was originally written as a defense of Parmenides' postulate that all movement is illusory. In its simplest form, Zeno's argument states that it is impossible for a man to cross a room, for in order to reach the far end, he must first reach the halfway point; however, once he makes it that far he must walk half the remaining distance, and then half the new remainder, and so forth, spawning an endless division of halves one could never succeed. Despite the obviously absurd conclusion, no one seemed capable of refuting it.

The Paradox of Motion, conceived by Zeno.

But as Western scholarship slowly became consumed by ecclesiastical dogma, the vast intellectual heritage of the Greeks was being absorbed and mastered by the Arabs. Having also adopted an improved number system from the Indians, Arab philosophers were better equipped to solve many of the prevailing ancient enigmas. Take another of Zeno's maddening arguments, the Achilles Paradox, which claims that a fast runner can never overtake a slower one, provided the latter has had even a slight headstart, because "the pursuer must first reach the point whence the pursued started," during which time the slower has advanced still farther, and so on, *ad infinitum*. The newly acquired concept of zero allowed this otherwise vicious regression of fractions to terminate at an absolute point, thereby revealing the fallacy laden in the riddle. Still, there were far more disquieting scenarios left by the ancients.

Enter: Hassan al Jafar, a 9th-century algorist determined to put an end to all "accursed insolubles." Al Jafar saw early on that at the heart of all absurdity lay the conflict between *actual* and *potential* infinity. This was the common thread, the central pillar upon which every known antinomy rested. Yet to refute limitlessness itself was equally foolish—ignoring the nonsensical because it was unwieldy did not make it go away. Instead, he sought a "mathematical elixir" which would neutralize ∞ by using its own powers against it.

His prescient solution to the Paradox of Motion was to introduce a competing paradox that immobilized the original. Simply put, one can cross a room if he travels at a fixed or increasing speed. Assuming,

Gregor Reisch, *Allegory of Arithmetic*, from "Margarita Philosophica" (1504).

as Zeno did, that each half-way point represents a task-in-itself, and that infinite "hyper-tasks" must be completed if one is to reach the wall, then one may also assume that, given a particular momentum, he may complete any number of hyper-tasks in pro-portionally diminishing intervals of time—simply adding them all up will result in a *finite* number:

$$1 + \frac{1}{2} + \frac{1}{4} + \frac{1}{8} + \frac{1}{16} \ldots = 2$$

In other words, a penny cut into infinite divisions still adds up to one cent.

But to the astonishment of his peers, al Jafar was not satisfied. There were other paradoxes, in fact infinite species of paradoxes, that would go unresolved indefinitely. "Merely pruning the leaves does not uproot the weed," he was known to grumble. The young algorist dreamed of producing a Metaparadox, a great and powerful formula which would contain the key to all possible paradoxes.

Like a diamond so resistant it may only be cut by another diamond, this algorithm would engender a *second* paradox, which would whittle down and ultimately negate the first. The principle was that the algebraic operations would locate the potential infinity and encode within it a reciprocal infinity moving in the opposite direction; the resulting interference would render each trajectory inert, and the two would snuff one another out like twin onrushing grass fires, extinguished by the others' ashes.

For decades, Hassan al Jafar chased the evanescent algorithm, his own white stag, through the thickets of recursive pattern and symbol. Only in his sickly, hobbling final years did he have a sudden awakening.

"I have crafted a most alluring proof!" he wrote to his former pupil, Abdul Zareh-Sharan. "Only, I fear there is far too little space to demonstrate here, for I have invented a novel language with which to express it."

By the time Zareh-Sharan had traveled across the Caspian Sea to receive his mentor's revelation, however, the master had expired, his monographs, draftworks and notebooks burned along with all his Earthly possessions in accordance with Hanabilite law.

It is not known whether al Jafar had truly succeeded in completing his magnum opus, but it is said that the story was woven into a Persian myth still honored by a remote fishing island off the coast of Mazandara. In the fable, a young prince is given a puzzle for his 18th birthday by a distant relative, but soon becomes so enchanted with the game that he forgets to age. Ironically, while the youth is bestowed with eternal life, he is deprived of the vital moments of which it is composed.

It is well known that abandoned subway and train stations abound in American cities, mosaics, columns. While the Library of Tangents celebrates these worthy achievements, to eras past.

The foundation to the demolished first court house (est. 1790), for instance, lies intact cement casings and rusty plumbing can be seen a wooden gallows from which the accused

Among the other forgotten artifacts are the Masonic burial grounds—catacombs bearing velvet armchairs and ornate, four-post beds, sealed off by a series of earthquakes which fiberglass cylinders so foreign-looking as to resemble an alien civilization.

There are also natural histories, geological histories-in-the-making, to be seen. Hollowed deposits, smatterings of iridescent quartz, sleek aluminum bricks, luminous spirals of bulbs of halite.

At certain points, it becomes difficult to distinguish between the natural and the The colorful swirls of minereal compounds, for example, can be mistaken for the bed of an molten alkalines.

Though some are disturbed by this eccentric interchangeability, it is precisely the sense evoke. Consider, for instance, the subject of the next exhibition: language.

---

some glorious remnants of prouder days, full of handsome WPA-commissioned murals,

equal emphasis is given to the lesser known, or in some cases, completely unknown testaments

just beneath the ground, above which currently is a parking lot. Through partially gutted once hung

the skeletons of high-ranking members in narrow shafts; an opulent gay brothel with plush

ravaged the land in the 17th century; and a strangely beautiful network of septic tanks, deep

cross-sections in the earth reveal marvelous structures of untouched limestone, rich calcium

phosphorous, crumpled sheets of granite, glimmering magnesium clusters, drippy white

industrial, and often too little information is provided to make a reasonable judgment.

old landfill, just as the heavy sludge of chemical waste might be confused with a tress of

of ambiguous estrangement, the rift between clarity and wonder, that the Library strives to

---

ULTIMA THULE

Languages of Hidden Islands

Johannes van Keulen, *Ries Palmers* (1753). Just as the Galapagos provided Charles Darwin a unique environment with which to observe the dynamics of competing species, so too do all isolated spaces offer ideal perspectives into the workings of nature, unencumbered by external influence. This exhibition examines several such "laboratories," wherein human languages have evolved or devolved in seclusion from the rest of the world.

LAND OF THE XHALAL

Approximately two hundred kilometers off the coast of Madagascar sits a small, nameless island marked by great volcanic masses and ribbed, lava-welded valleys. The mostly parched stretch of earth is populated by a small tribe known as the Xhalal. Almost nothing has been written about them, but the small bit that is known is wondrous. They are perhaps the only people in history to speak in sign despite flawless hearing. Even today, they occupy a culture of silence for what might be termed religious beliefs, though the precise reasons are unclear. Like most belief systems, their mythology presumes the existence of a family of creators, and that these gods communicate with one another and to man through some transcendent means beyond words. To worship them, to obtain divine wisdom, the Xhalal believe, one must abandon verbal signifiers and communicate through a pure *lingua franca*. From this the first sign language was born.

However, over the centuries it was noticed that even the most plainly "iconistic" gestures (raising the index finger to denote the number one, rubbing the stomach to indicate hunger), were becoming truncated and foreshortened as well, a process known as "co-articulation." The Xhalal then decided that each generation would reinvent its lexicon for the next, in order to keep its morphology fresh and simple. But even these signs became corrupted and abused within a matter of years or even months. The moment children became fluent in the new language—remarkably fast—the symbols were almost immediately simplified and "slurred" into abstraction, and often further altered with accompanying sounds—verbal phonemes, clicks, snaps, claps, stomps, etc. In short, the language became formalized.

Presumably, the gods did not communicate with one another through a construction of any kind, so the Xhalal decreed that in order to harmonize with the earth and the sea and the heavens, they must communicate directly, without recourse to any manufactured tongue. So the Xhalal took a vow of deep silence—no words, no pictures, no signs, gestures or symbols. No lexicon, no grammar. No signifiers, no representations. They would simply live among the pure forms of nature. Fire was fire. Rain was rain. A cool breeze was not wind, for each shift of air pressure was its own entity. There was no generalizing, no grouping, no species or phyla. A sea turtle was not *a* sea turtle but *that* sea turtle and no other.

A traveler may be awestruck by the Xhalal's silence. How is it that they are able to live and work and procreate? How can they possibly get along without at least a common system of reference? How do they know when it's time to hunt or feed the children, or warn one another of an invading tribe?

The answer is that they do, though the traveler may be blind to it. In fact, the Xhalal themselves may not realize it, but they are communicating as eloquently as with any other language through minute, practically invisible cues. Just as slight variations in intonation may indicate completely different concepts in Mandarin, here the rapid blink of an eye means something very different than a slightly less rapid blink. Pinched lips indicate a particular shade of jealousy while pursed lips expresses schadenfreude. Even a syntax has emerged unconsciously through the otherwise imperceptible flexings of cheek muscles, which are necessary to understand tenses and causality.

As far as the Xhalal are concerned, however, they speak the language of the gods.

OAXAXGHANA

Toward the northwestern tip of Micronesia is a tiny archipelago ravaged by geothermal waste and fallout from nearby nuclear test sites. These desiccated patches of land make up the Oaxaxghana ["wah-hä-ZHON-uh"] islands, described by ecologists as some of the most nightmarish wastelands in the biosphere.

Skies in this region are jaundiced from successive waves of rising radioactive gas. Vegetation is scarce: Trees are leafless and wiry and low to the ground, the ferns are of a fried-looking, brownish purple variety, the narrow spectrum of edible fruits have a disconcertingly malty aftertaste. Air is almost sulfuric— stale and tangy and overwarm, like the breath of a flu-ridden child.

What remains unknown to researchers, because most refuse to step foot on this toxic earth, is that a community of Oaxaxghanese continue to populate the islands, living in shallow caves like prehistoric scavengers. It is said of them that, in contrast to their congenitally colorblind neighbors in Pingelap, they suffer from *hyperchromatopsia*, a rare neuro-optical phenomenon afflicting subjects with an extreme hypersensitivity to colors.

Primary and secondary tones in particular are perceived by the Oaxaxghanese as blindingly vivid, supersaturated. Flickering

36

candlelight appears as vibrant as a flashing police siren; a pair of blue eyes looks as full and lustrous as a storm-swept sky. Something as simple as flint rock gleams as brightly as a camera flash. The abundance of color is incapacitating, hallucinatory. To stare at the sparkling sea is suicide. This is why the Oaxaxghanese hunt at night and confine their daily activities to caves.

Some say that with this burden comes a terrific advantage. Just as the blind may develop compensatory enhancements in other senses, the Oaxaxghanese are able to see beyond the ordinary visual spectrum into the secret realm of invisible hues and particles that covertly permeate our world. Shadows are rich with detail. What is, to us, a starless sky, is, to them, a cavern of shimmering minerals. Tree bark is alive with violets and silvers and crystalline beads of sap. The blurry waves of heat one sees rising from a fire, or the steam one exhales into the freezing night air, mark the extremes of what ordinary humans are able to perceive, whereas the *hyperchromatopsiac* can read the fine textures embedded in thermal events—smudgy auras radiating off of flesh, schools of refracted light rays through glass. A minor static discharge to us—an imperceptible spark of electricity thrown from wool sheets or a metal doorknob—is, to them, a splendid miniature lightning storm.

This receptivity affords the Oaxaxghanese a vocabulary marvelously abundant with color labels. Just as certain Amazonian tribes are able to identify up to eight distinct quarter tones inside a half-step of Western harmony, the islanders see dozens of shades lurking in the cracks between azure and magenta, teal and cyan. *Urük* indicates a class of colors between nickel and zinc; *juipuo* marks a place halfway between gold and bronze.

It is unknown precisely what events led to this neuro-chromatic curiosity, though botanists have identified a particular cycad, for centuries a staple of the Oaxaxghanese diet, which had adapted to the harsh conditions of the radiation fallout, and now yields toxic seeds.

THE FIFTH ISLAND OF JAPAN

Many are familiar with the four central islands: Hokkaido, Honshu, Shikoku and Kyushu, which make up the "mainland" of Japan proper. However, there are over 2,000 smaller islands that go largely unnoticed by the rest of the world—among them Nyogima, home to a once-renowned maritime village toward the far north.

Kawanabe Kyosai, Ink sketches for two horizontal panel paintings of crows (c. 1885).

There was much to admire about this isolated culture, which had developed a sophisticated infrastructure independent of its neighbors—paved roads, irrigation systems, boats, ports, bridges—

as well as advanced medicine, telescopes, hunting weapons and a rich literary tradition dating back to the 12th century.

One unfortunate shortcoming, however, was the island's failure to erect a hurricane barrier. A cataclysmic tsunami swept the land some two hundred years ago, annihilating schools, museums, libraries and businesses, not to mention thousands of lives. Tablets were shattered, scrolls soaked through, gardens upended, temples pulled asunder. All that was left from the rubble lay inside the heads of the island's inhabitants—their folklore, their music, their stories—a fading collective memory of a lacerated civilization.

The Nyogimians assumed the gods had punished them for their pride and their reliance upon material goods. Consequently, the Reconstruction Committee resolved that their history, so sacred to them—half-remembered, half-imagined—would now rely on a purely oral tradition, lest they remain susceptible to future loss. The people would carry their heritage from one generation to the next without the help of engravings or architecture or complex tools—all of these perishable, illusory. What was real was the carriage of time itself, the experience of a people.

Gradually, a new order was borne from the waste. Drawing from a long tradition of Kodo drumming, the Nyogimians possessed a large vocabulary of rhythms, which they were able to translate into codifiers for actions and qualities. Just as their formerly organized society had been washed and battered together in the wreckage, texts, dialects and music began to merge into a unified language of patterns. Soon, these intricate phonemic strings were capable of expressing as many concepts as their previous language, perhaps more. All linguistic information—

gender, interrogatives, tenses, etc.—could be communicated by a system of metric and notational values.

Their monosyllabic tongue, having emerged from Kodo, is essentially binary like Morse code and is organized by the division between "long" sounds (1/4 notes) and "short" sounds (1/8 notes). However, its inflections are denoted by a subsystem of accents, time signatures, repetitions, plus a small body of phonemic variations.

	Subject	Quality	Action	Tense	Object
Meaning	I, You, It	Hot, Cold, Hunger	See, Want, Have	Past, Pres., Fut.	Food, Water
Notational Transliteration	1st Beat, 2nd Beat, 3rd Beat	Triplets, Dotted 8th Notes, 16th Notes	Cha, Po, Di	6/8, 4/4, 5/4	Twice, Three Times
Element	Accent	Value/Pattern	Phoneme	Meter	Repetition

Nyogimian relies on a highly elaborated system of prosody—patterns of rhythm and sound. It should be noted that other linguistic information such as number and aspect is delivered by subtleties in intonation, vowel length and reduplication of the stem. For instance, *cha* is "to see" but *chaaa* is "seeing *over some period of time*."

To a visitor, a conversation may sound like organized gibberish, nonlinguistic. Yet he would be foolish to dismiss this toneless chanting as nonsensical. When the Nyogimians communicate, they gesticulate, interrupt one another, laugh, grunt, nod—in effect, they behave like any other culture does when talking.

What is genuinely befuddling and alien, however, are social events. Should you witness a heated discussion or an argument among a group of men, you will hear the most splendid suffusion of rhythms and tones—dizzying rapid-fire chains of percussive utterances, interlocking and syncopated and completely spontaneous. The tempo remains curiously constant among the group despite the phenomenal variation in pattern and meter. Like synchronizing menstrual cycles, Nyogimian speech patterns unconsciously gravitate toward one another, attuning themselves in time.

But even this speaks nothing of what one beholds during a wild boar hunt or a fire dance or a sacrifice. Stacked polyrhythms chatter through the woods, microtones shift back and forth as the pack proceeds, dividing and regrouping.

For the Nyogimians, music and meaning are one.

FAIRØS

Like the mythical forest hut of the infamous Russian succubus, Baba Yaga, which sits perched on hens' legs so that it may shift locations through the night, Fairøs is a mobile island, variously appearing and vanishing about the Arctic Circle. What had bewildered explorers and cartographers until fairly recently was that Fairøs was—and still is—a giant glacier floating between Iceland and Greenland.

The climatological "mixing zone" that characterizes the high arctic—warm currents from the Gulf Stream meeting frigid polar winds—allows for a nutrient-rich ecology. A vast tundra of knotted lichens and white mosses is cut by coiled rivulets of ice, alternately freezing and thawing. Forbs and sedges form a muted brown-grey patchwork along the coastline. As the land is not technically land at all, there are no deep root systems and hence very little greenery, unlike the mainlands which flank it.

By default, the inhabitants of Fairøs are something of a nomadic tribe, living off of gulls and trout and the booty of sailors—an island of pirates. They are a diminutive, muscular people with angular, Teutonic faces and gleaming black eyes.

One theory holds that the glacier was once connected to the Eastern fjords of Iceland and gradually broke off sometime between the 11th and 12th centuries, carrying a small band of Vikings who refused to part from their homeland. But something curious, and perhaps inevitable, happened over the course of the next few decades. Items that had initially passed as currency—fox pelts, crowberries, Barite crystals and other goods with some nominal measure of intrinsic worth, were no longer available. The eagles' beaks had snapped, the sheepdog scalps had decomposed and fallen apart, and rather than revert to barter (which was seen as Plebian), they elected to invent a new currency, a representation of value in lieu of actual value.

So they started drawing. The tundra yielded enough plant fibers to grind a plentiful supply of paper and enough lichens for purple dyes. Soon, teams of artisans had formed a "mint," which produced carefully rendered images of skins and gems, each denoting a particular "amount," and circulated these chits within the community. They were essentially IOUs to be redeemed for actual goods looted from sailors—wool, weapons, lumber. Again, inevitably, the looters over the years gained enough of a reserve to issue promissory notes to merchants and craftsmen, which spawned a culture based entirely on faith, of promises and promises of promises. And as the backings were gradually withdrawn or abandoned, to the point where credit slips were five and six generations removed from the material items they initially represented, this enumeration of symbols began to influence the Fairøs language.

Centuries had passed since any living islander had seen an actual fox or a gazelle or a tree, or heard the clanking of a well or read the *Prose Edda*, and yet these words, or traces of these words, persisted through the ages. The origins no longer mattered. They may as well never have existed. Just as whale teeth and puffin wings had lost their monetary significance, words, which had stood for concepts and classes of *things*, in their absence became abstracted into *qualities*. For instance, Loki, the Norse trickster god of yore, might have been discarded over the years as a religious presence and yet was preserved in some variation as a signifier of duplicity.

Virtually the entire Fairøs language was simply the pulp of what its speakers had managed to scavenge from the high seas. Treasures they'd pirated—strange gleaming metals, magic discs with arrows that always pointed in the same direction, snarling four-legged creatures—were each individually named, and as time passed and these things grew scarce, their signifiers were inflated, generalized and/or corrupted to fit a linguistic need, or else abandoned and left to oblivion.

Unanchored by geography or tradition, Fairøs consumes its own history. Fairøs culture, like currency itself, is a nest of fictions—there is no standard, no material to fall back on. Even numbers have little value any longer; meaning is no longer in things or even in concepts of things, but in the syntax, the act of transaction.

SANTANZES

The *Hand of Satan*, as it was known to the Spanish, was associated for many centuries with myths inherited from the ancient mariners, who believed the island to possess demonic properties. Explorers who'd traveled west of Fernandina to Santanzes and experienced its otherworldly ambiance—the inebriating humidity, the loamy marshlands, the great peacock-like birds flaring radiant feathered wings and grotesque, fist-sized insects darting through the air with buzzing shrieks, the fields of shoulder height, the geysers belching foul gasses, the walnut-skinned Indians—returned with inexplicable diseases and spoke feverishly before their deaths of sudden visions and memories blooming before them like living dreams.

These tales only deepened the mainlanders' superstitions of a satanic presence. Many believed the island itself to possess a single living consciousness, taking the form of a giant sea turtle or pirãnha whose terrible head would emerge from the sea and devour passing ships from beneath. Unsuspecting sailors would be lured by the hypnotic sweep of the equatorial sun as it blazed over the cerulean water only to be swallowed whole by a mythical beast. Those not attacked directly were believed to have been intoxicated by its primordial breath.

There is, at least, a metaphoric truth to these myths. A great

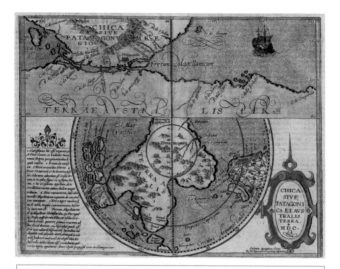

Leen Helmink, *Chica sive Patagonica et Australis Terra* (1608). "*Terra Australus Incognita*," Latin for "the unknown land of the South," appears on countless maps between the 15th and 18th centuries.

epidemic befell the Santanzese sometime during the late 16th century. Those that were spared experienced not light-headedness or high fever or dizziness or any typical symptoms of infection, but rather an incapacitating *acuity* of memory. Or, more accurately, an inability to forget.

It would seem that, as maladies go, one could do worse than a photographic memory. But for a moment, imagine every trivial fragment of even one day's worth of experience occupying a place in your mind. Your grocery bill. The obligatory chitchat with your neighbor. The incessant background prattle of radio personalities. The cover of every item at the newsstand. The financing rates of every car you do not want. Imagine every beat of existence swallowed and inscribed forever in your brain.

A team of pathologists and anthropologists had gotten wind

of this curious phenomenon in the 1960s and ventured to see if the rumors were true. They subjected the Santanzese to a series of rigorous tests—general performance exams such as being asked to recall strings of words and numbers—and were unable to place a limit on their memory. Entire pages of alphanumeric code could be recalled verbatim not only moments later but hours, days, weeks and months later, with no discernable decline in performance whatsoever.

The findings ushered in a wave of interest from specialists around the world, particularly evolutionary biologists and historians. However, it was soon discovered that to complete a history of the Santanzes would be like Achilles catching up to the tortoise. A single tribesman's testimony would take as many days to recount as it had taken to live.

The Santanzese themselves, of course, have no use for books. Elsewhere on the globe, texts—all texts—were initially devised to ease the burden of memory by recording measured units, plots of land, livestock, debts and interest rates, sacks of barley and corn, etc., but what use would such numerical records have to a culture of mnemonics? Unfortunately, that most significant by-product of print, that ill-defined afterthought which serves universally as a barometer of cultivation and refinement—literature—remains absent among the Santanzese. Necessity begets invention, as the saying goes; without it, nothing can evolve.

Not that they would have anything to write about if they could. Imagination and the telling of narratives require as much forgetting as remembering, as much dullness as sharpness. The storyteller must select among the moments he is recounting. He must smudge details, distort time and sequence, ignore the irrelevant, embellish and fabricate. Borges reminds us that without the ability to generalize, to extract similarities from apparently different things, there is no abstraction, and hence no thought.

Does it follow, paradoxically, that despite their bottomless reservoir of memory, the Santanzese are incapable of reflection?

Some say there is no Library, that it is merely an elaborate hoax. They claim that images of various theatrical sets, and the train is nothing but a form of cinema. But if this "filmmakers," who have so effectively illusioned their viewers like magicians.

Still others believe that the Library's intentions are more suspicious; that the low that they misinterpret as real. The skeptics say the Library capitalizes on the insecurities clandestine knowledge of which the vast majority is deprived.

As if in response to its critics, half mocking, half humoring, the Library has

the subways never leave their stations, that the windows are in fact screens which display

were true, then one's sense of wonder only shifts to the masterful work of the curators, or

oxygen levels in the abandoned subway system cause people to have euphoric visions

of its viewers, who desperately wish to believe in secrets, to believe that they are privy to a

presented an exhibition of secrecy itself in the Hall of Vanishing Manuscripts . . .

PARABLEPSIS

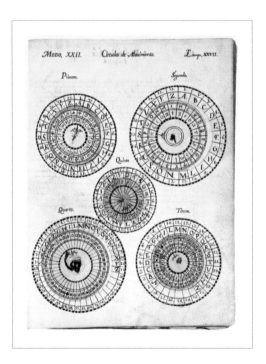

Vanishing Manuscripts

Anon., *Cryptographic wheels* (1647). Like the spoken word, text was borne of the necessity to communicate information, though it had the advantage of doing so across space and time. But while some writings were widely and publicly distributed, others contained information intended only for selected readers and thus had to be encrypted. These reciprocal efforts to conceal and reveal are but two sides of the same coin, and together comprise the history of print.

THE MERCURIAL CODEX

The early days of Christianity were rife with difficulties, the most intractable of which being the internal struggle to define what the religion was in the first place. No one could seem to agree on the "original" teachings of Christ, nor his alleged divinity, let alone the torrent of interpretations that followed.

The Docetics believed that Jesus was God himself, but only *appeared* to look like a man; the Ebionites held the "adoptionist" conviction that he was a common, flesh-and-blood mortal who merely acted in a divine manner; the Gnostics testified that there were no fewer than ten gods; others believed in two—one God of the Old Testament and one of the New; still others believed in a single, all powerful Creator. For the first four centuries, Christianity was its own Tower of Babel, desperately struggling to communicate with itself.

Another challenge was finding a dependable technique with which to disseminate the scriptures from one community to another. Most Christians were illiterate and had to rely on a limited group of leaders to interpret and facilitate the sacred rites, rules and distributions of power among the church. The scriptures themselves, however, were the product of generations of scribes who had, intentionally or not, altered the texts.

As Christianity spread, more texts naturally required copy-

copying, but the more copies were made, the more errors would arise. Some were deliberate—scribes would sometimes change a word or a line to shift its theological or liturgical implications—but far more were trivial. All the early Greek texts were written in *scriptio continua*, a linked, cursive-like technique devoid of punctuation or spaces between words, which, not surprisingly, allowed for frequent mistakes in both

Anon. MS. 1370, fol. 172r. *The Macdurnan Gospels* (9th century).

reading and transcription. An abbreviation of one word could be misinterpreted by another scribe as a full word. And in an age preceding that of mechanical reproduction, each alteration became permanent—a simple spelling mistake or slip of the pen in the copying of scripture was now itself *part* of that scripture—so long as it was not subsumed by another error.

All of this was exacerbated by the escalating competition between sects. It was not uncommon for scribes to pseudonymously attribute their words to Paul or another apostle, thereby lending authority to their own particular views. Therefore, in an effort to protect themselves from the increasing number of forgeries, stricter protocols were adopted. The Corinthians would warn against the "false teachings" of the Galatians in a letter, which would itself be copied and corrupted. Many of these epistles were collected and bound together into sacred codices, but as each new addition was added, the number of inconsistencies grew.

Fed up with the ever-mounting fallacies permeating all of Christendom, a small group of Locrinthian scholars decided to put a stop to it. After a period of rather hazardous chemical experimentation, they succeeded in devising a method of preserving and reproducing their most reliable texts is such a way as to shield them indefinitely from further tampering. The procedure began by forging a mastertext whose letters were painted onto a vellum scroll with a hot gelatinous substrate, which congealed into a protruding typeface. Once cool, the embossed document could then be reproduced in facsimile form through simple charcoal rubs. If copyists did so carefully, no further truths would be lost in translation.

What was not known, however, was that the metallic dye was highly toxic. The compound, now suspected to be mercury-based, slowly and invisibly began to leak through the scroll and into each subsequent rubbing. (The more the text was agitated, the warmer and less stable the solution became.) It is likely that everyone who touched the scripts became intoxicated with their poison, and as Locrinthia lacked an updated irrigation system, it was not long before the commoners, too, were exposed.

Symptoms emerged gradually: among them dizziness, ear-ringing, swollen lymph nodes; but the most common and difficult to treat was memory loss. Like modern-day Alzheimer's disease, it usually began as general forgetfulness and diminishing short-term recall, but eventually crystallized into full-blown amnesia. Within a single season, the epidemic had spread through all of

Locrinthia. Citizens were forced to wear muzzles and gloves; neighboring towns cut off all trade relations for fear of welcoming the dreaded *veninum ex deus*.

One can only imagine the strangeness of everyday life. Familiar things—people, places, one's own history—were becoming increasingly foreign. A certain listless opacity had fallen like a veil between the afflicted and the world beyond; the daily checks and measures of existence were smearing into an anesthetized haze. But while the Locrinthians failed to remember the names of their wives and children, they'd also forgotten their enemies, their harbored resentments. Indeed all the animosities and feelings of ill-will that had once plagued them evaporated into a fine mist. All were bestowed with a blank slate, wiped clear each day. Departed friends were no longer mourned. Distinctions between the affluent and the destitute faded.

The Locrinthians lost the ability to recite the scriptures, to observe the rules and to carry forth the teachings of their savior, and yet for the duration of their short lives, each citizen was redeemed.

CYANOTYPOGRAPHY

The flip side of making texts legible and accessible to all was the concurrent struggle to keep others hidden from view. "Disappearing" and "reappearing" messages have indeed enjoyed a long and largely inscrutable history. As late as the 16th century, an Italian scientist named Giovanni Porta (not to be confused with the 18th-century opera composer), described how to conceal a message within a hardboiled egg. (First, he instructed, mix one ounce of alum with one pint of vinegar. Next, dip the stem of a feather into the solution and write

Camillo Camilli, *Imprese Ilustri di diversi* (1586). A 16th-century cipher wheel.

a message onto the surface of an egg. The ink will then penetrate the porous shell, leaving the inscription on the hardened egg beneath, which can only be read once the shell has been peeled.)

Pliny the Elder related a similar technique in the 1st century, only his invisible ink was extracted from a thithymallus plant and written neatly onto papyrus. This was less time-consuming than tattooing the text onto a messenger's shaven head and waiting for his hair to grow back, and certainly less cumbersome than scrunching the message into a ball of wax and swallowing it. A relatively recent version of this tactic was employed in WWI, when German agents would photographically shrink an entire message to the size of a period and then hide this tiny, slightly shiny dot in the text of an apparently unexceptional letter. The receiver would simply slide his hands over the paper to find the telltale slipperiness of a photographic emulsion, then read it under a microscope.

These types of practices all fall under the category of *steganography*, meaning hidden, as distinct from *cryptography*, meaning encoded. The first ciphers proper—that is, messages whose contents are disguised by scrambling their constituent symbols— were set to use by the Spartans around 400 B.C.E., though *cryptanalysis*—the study of decipherment—did not begin for at least another thousand years.

The Arabian manuscript *On Deciphering Cryptographic Messages* by the philosopher al-Kindi contained a solution to what was thought to be an unbreakable code. The once-ironclad substitution cipher worked like any modern children's cryptogram in that each letter of the plaintext was substituted for another. For instance, one could encode a document by replacing every *A* with a *Z*, every *B* with a *Y*, every *C* with an *X*, and so forth. Encrypting the word *UNBREAKABLE* would thusly result in *FMYIVZPZYOV*. As long as the key was unknown, the ciphertext would remain indecipherable. Al-Kindi, however, found that by simply calculating the frequency with which each letter appeared in the encrypted text, and then comparing those numbers to the frequency with which each letter arose in the language at-large, the key would reveal itself.

Letter	Percentage	Letter	Percentage
A	8.2	N	6.7
B	1.5	O	7.5
C	2.8	P	1.9
D	4.3	Q	.1
E	12.7	R	6
F	2.2	S	6.3
G	2	T	9.1
H	6.1	U	2.8
I	7	V	1
J	.2	W	2.4
K	.8	X	2
L	4	Y	2
M	2.4	Z	.1

The general frequency with which the letters of the alphabet occur in English-language texts. Abu-Yusuf Ya `qoub ibn `Ishaq ibn al-Sabbah ibn `Omran ibn Isma `il al-Kindi was the first to suggest that by comparing the statistical frequency of the letters within a language at-large to the scrambled letters in a particular mono-alphabetic substitution cipher, the encoded message could be deciphered.

In many ways, the history of encryption is also the story of science and mathematics, to say nothing of military strategy, behavioral psychology and other fields. Innovation often arrives by setting a practical goal and becoming distracted along the way. But lacking immediate utilitarian use, many otherwise critical advances were lost because their application was overlooked.

One such case involves the brief practice of so-called cyanotypography, which was employed by Chinese spies during the Song Dynasty. Increasingly suspicious of the looming Jurchins, the military commander Yue Fei dispatched waves of secret agents to retrieve information from the court of Jin in order to prepare for any forthcoming invasion. The Song Dynasty was the most technologically sophisticated society the Eastern World had ever seen—rich with goods and materials, among them gunpowder, ploughs, hammers, needles and the first paper money printed by a moveable-type press—and would have made for a most desirable conquest.

The preternaturally intuitive Yue Fei sought to protect his homeland by gathering as much information as he could about the neighboring kingdoms without their knowledge. One such strategy was to print instructions to his spies with disappearing ink so that, if caught, the enemy would be unable to decipher the message. Unfortunately, his enemies were discovering the secret solutions on their own, and began routinely subjecting all suspicious documents to applications of lemon juice and heat. If a military order was discovered, the spy was pumped for information and promptly disemboweled.

One day, an aging typesetter named Zhao Xi approached the general with an intriguing idea. By concocting a recipe of ferric ammonium citrate and potassium ferricyanide, then soaking a printing ribbon with the solution, a magical, "self-destructing" text could be produced. *Show me*, said Yue Fei. Zhao Xi promptly composed a legible document printed on a sheet of fine silk and bequeathed it to the general. In three days, the information had vanished without a trace, only to reappear once enclosed in darkness. When asked how this mysterious chemical worked its magic, Zhao Xi explained that the compound was light-sensitive; that it revealed itself by absorbing sun rays, but was quick to fade unless stored in a contained environment.

What he did not realize was that the bluish silver solution was capable of capturing subtle ratios of shadows-to-luminosity if placed inside a pin-pricked box or camera obscura. But the desire to accurately depict reality was not yet a priority for the Chinese, nor even a particularly attractive concept—beauty existed in nature and in artistic renderings of it, not cheap simulacra. When the Jurchins did finally invade, the laboratories were burned along with the temples, the libraries and the farms—and the secrets of cyanotypography would no longer see the light of day.

BOOK OF GLASS

The great scope of narrative form has undergone innumerable permutations since its first flickerings in the human
imagination, though it is possible to observe a general shape or
constellation that has etched itself out over time. It should be no
surprise, for instance, that as language evolved, the stories men
told grew from simple confabulations ("here is how I caught this
deer . . .") and primitive extrapolations ("this is why lightning
strikes . . .") to elaborate and wondrous tales meant to edu-
cate, enlighten and amuse. But the rest of the world was evolv-
ing as well, and the content of these tales shifted to reflect man's
changing appetites and fears.

The earliest surviving fictions reveal an overwhelming preoccupation with cosmogony. Gods and other intervening celestial
agents were the focus of man's attention—the vast majority of
songs, epics, folktales and myths concerned the origins of the
universe and the forces believed to be responsible. This gave way
during the late Renaissance to an interest in culture, in man's
self-created world of rules and conventions, the structure of
society, the flow of capital, the institutions which allocate power.
If gods or demons appeared, they were incidental to the action,
not elemental to it.

The next major epoch sought to examine the mind, the

Karaite Bible, Bound manuscript (10th century). The British Library. ELS2006.3.37

organ that perceived and measured the external world. For these writers, society only existed insofar as it was impressed upon the individual. This fascination with the subjective reached its culmination with the modernists, and was soon followed by an interest in what the mind *produced*—namely, narrative form itself. And for the greater part of the past century, so-called post-modernists have remained enchanted by the technique of art-making, by the puzzling and uniquely human craft of recomposing our experience of reality through artifice.

One peculiar narrative, a 1,200-odd page Japanese text, may have clairvoyantly anticipated all of this.

Little is known about this novel. The last surviving copy was stolen from the Österreichische Nationalbibliothek in Vienna in 1977, so we must resort to the body of literature written about it (and plagiarized from it) in the years subsequent to its printing. Written by an unknown poet in the 9th century, *Lady Makura and the Book of Glass* tells the story of a powerful but dim-witted lord whose young concubine steals away every night with a different lover. Suspicious, he demands of her an explanation and each morning she concocts a new tale of her nocturnal adventures to placate him. Her impromptu fictions comprise the body of the text.

It is not clear how many stories the *Book of Glass* contains— there are suspected to be hundreds, if not thousands—but reports indicate that they are marked by multifarious uses of printsetting, typography and narrative technique.

One parable describes a monk with lofty dreams of attaining ultimate wisdom. Every day he climbs higher up a mountain, and every evening prays to the Earth God for the peak to rise so that he may reach the moon. But as the story goes on, the size of the text grows ever smaller, so that by the end, we, the reader, have no idea what becomes of him. We are left as blind as the monk and his ill-fated quest.

In "Han-Su and the Magic Mirror," a village girl proves so generous and kind that her image in a pocket mirror remains beautiful even as she, herself, ages. To read the story, however, the reader must procure a mirror of his own, as the text is printed backwards.

Similarly, in "The Prophetic Cherry Tree," the form is inextricable from the content. A child prince plants a cherry seed which grows into a magnificent tree. After many years of tending it, the prince awakens one morning to find that its leaves have fallen in a pattern that spells a message—a warning that his pernicious brother plans to betray him in order to inherit the throne. Only once the reader has finished the story is he informed that the paper on which it had been written was pulped from those very leaves.

Other tales incorporated etchings and engravings, rhymed couplets, theatrical dialogues, taxonomies, even secret pockets and collapsed predellas, each device customized to serve the particular theme. One was a murder mystery that only revealed the killer once its final page was folded into an origami pattern. Another was said to have contained only blank pages intended for the reader to imprint with his own story.

What strikes us today is not simply the virtuosic technical and literary skill with which the tales were composed, but the almost sibylline way the book's architecture foreshadowed the course of future storytelling. The first of the *Lady Makura* stories describe celestial doings—divinations, supernatural encounters—the second group restrict themselves to society—manners, traditions of civility—the next concern the interior life of the narrator herself—dreams, ruminations, desires—and finally, the last focus on language—the nature of organized symbols and their ability or inability to convey meaning.

Yet questions abound. We are not sure to what extent, if at all, the elusive manuscript was a compendium of preexisting myths. Were any based in historical fact? Was the unknown poet really a single writer or an amalgam of many? We do know that the text has itself attained legendary status among bibliophiles. Some say it contains lysergic residue that inebriates the reader, making him so mesmerized that he can never read the same story twice. Readers with mystical inclinations believe that the text contorts itself to suit each reader, such that each tale is a reflection of his individual situation, like the *I-Ching*. Whatever the case, one can only hope that in time the *Book of Glass* will turn up in the black market unshattered.

Some of the Library's greatest and most haunting sights are those that lie deep beneath the

which a glimmering subaqueous world becomes visible. Some riverbeds are bejeweled with

oars, wristwatches, tarnished handmirrors, deteriorating dolls, faded magazines, the shells

You will pass over and between functioning railroad tunnels, seaweed-entwined bridge

Most mystifying, perhaps, are the remnants of a large, sunken barge from the 1920s.

accessories have remained curiously ordered along the floor. The plates and silverware lie

upright, undisturbed, though the racks have dissolved. A row of life jackets rest symmetrically

capsized.

Experts continue to debate the likelihood that such items could stay so miraculously

claim that the Library stages these items with the intention of manipulating its passengers

impossible nor even particularly unlikely.

Even these controversial wonders, however, pale to the breathtaking items you are

surface of rivers, ponds and reservoirs. Certain tracks are housed by translucent tunnels through

stones and scampering crustaceans, others with lost items from above—submerged canoe

of roman candles—variously buried and unearthed as the sandy floor shifts.

pilings, rocky caves, swaying faunal gardens, schools of undulating jellyfish.

Though the masts and hull panels have decomposed and split, many of the boat's onboard

perfectly stacked, though the cupboards have long since vanished; passengers' luggage sits

against one another exactly as they'd been arranged in the emergency chest before the boat

well-preserved under thousands of pounds of water and the influence of heavy tides. Critics

into believing such phenomena possible, while others rebuff that the alternative is neither

exposed to in the Microbes Wing . . .

MICROGRAPHIA ESOTERICA

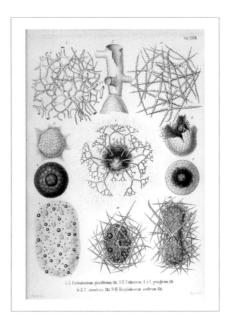

The Hypothetical Ancestors of Ernst Haeckel

Ernst Haeckel, *Die Radiolarien* (1862). Before the 17th century, infectious disease, mold, pond scum—all were assumed to have arisen from ill-defined, spontaneous means, or by the hand of a supernatural agent, until Anton van Leeuwenhoek peered through a disc of concave glass and glimpsed an infinitesimal universe rife with alien creatures. The "animalcules" he described recalled a theory—if such a term applies—proposed by a Roman writer named Varro in the 1st century B.C.E., that illness resulted from the inhalation of "tiny beasts." But while modern science has equipped us with a proper germ theory of disease, we remain flummoxed by the complexity of these "beasts" and their evolutionary ancestry.

I

The number of microorganic species which had come and gone in the roughly two billion years between the first bacteria on Earth and the first multicellular animals is incalculable. What properties did these hapless beings possess? Did the primordial atmosphere equip certain germs with radiation-resistant membranes only to leave them vulnerable to the forthcoming oxygen? Did they scutter about the blazing deserts like crabs or confine themselves to the ocean's depths? Did they feast on carbon residue in volcanic hollows or sulfur deposits pluming from hydrothermal vents?

We cannot presume to know. Microbial life comes in such staggering variety that almost no mutative possibility can be ruled out. We've seen archaea thrive under extreme barometric pressure, halophiles tolerate the saltiest waters, hyperthermophiles excell in temperatures exceeding 230° F. Some aquatic species produce methane that bubbles up to the ocean's surface and can be ignited by a bolt of lightning—others *eat* methane. Some microbes control their buoyancy, and thus their depth in the water, through internal gas bubbles. Others are airborne, capable of propelling themselves aloft with vibrating flagella.

Only recently did we become aware that microbes predate human beings by untold eons, that they outnumber the cells in our own bodies by a factor of ten, that they will outlive all other life on the planet by millions of years.

The intimate mechanics of microbes continue to elude many of the world's greatest researchers. It may be said that, if we are largely ignorant of the vast majority of life which exists today, we are manifestly ignorant of that which existed in the past.

II

Our knowledge of prehistoric microbiology comes mostly from specimens found preserved in rocks, ice or from insects trapped in sap. Chemolithotrophic, or "rock-eating" bacteria, have been discovered in Basalt deposits 4,700 feet underground in solid rock. A 250-million-year-old germ, *Bacillus permians*, was siphoned from salt crystals buried in a New Mexico cavern and reanimated.

In 1996, the largest bacterium ever thought to exist was found fossilized within the liver of a petrified goat. Dubbed the *pantaphile*, the cell body of this mammoth cylindrical germ was measured to be over two feet long. Previous to this, the largest bacteria were believed to be the *thiomargarita namibiensis* or "sulfur pearl of Namibia," which range from 100 to 750 micrometers.

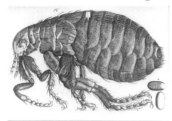

Philippus Bonanni, *Observationes circa viventia, quæ in rebus non viventibus reperiuntur: Cum micrographia curiosa* (1691).

On the opposite extreme is a species so miniscule its existence is only theoretical. Referred to by microbiologists as "particle bacteria," these nano-scale germs arise through a quantum condition known as entanglement, a spooky phenomenon wherein two mirror-image particles become indistinguishable, despite being separated by space. In a sense, they are one—a single body existing in two distinct places at the same time.

Once entangled, the particles will henceforth be impossible to tease apart because their characteristics are now identical. In fact, changing the state of one inevitably and instantaneously affects the state of the other. This means that a change in one bacterium hosted by a cow in Kansas could alter the state of its entangled twin inside a puffin in Reykjavík.

III

Other microbes are more remarkable for their behavior than their size. Metuspores, for instance—named after the Latin root *metus* meaning "dread" or "anxiety"—were a family of bacteria discovered by the Swiss physician, Dr. René Droz, following a sudden outbreak of a typhus variant in 1947. The disease, which was distinguished by plague-like boils, high fever and intermittent delirium, had developed the reputation of being transmitted through fear. Droz considered this urban legend to be not far from the truth.

In the medical community, the theory seemed at best highly speculative and at worst fatuous and irresponsible. True, the afflicted were almost exclusively anxious types, temperamentally fretful, even hypochondriacal, but was that alone cause for such a far-fetched hypothesis? "Not necessarily," wrote Droz. "It is not uncommon in the natural world for a predator to sense the fear of its prey. Is it so unthinkable that this character might also apply to the micrographic?" Droz went on to cite dozens of instances wherein certain organisms displayed signs of fear—smells, changes in pigment, etc.—that predators had adapted to perceive. His conviction, in the case of the metuspore, was that the aggressive microbes were attracted to a "nervous frequency" unwittingly emitted by their jittery prey.

Droz tested this theory in a laboratory by subjecting a vial of spores to a spectrum of high-frequency electrical waves. Lo and behold, when exposed to a particular bandwidth, the bacteria mobilized. He conjectured that the frequency originated from a "fear center" in the human brain, which acted as a homing signal for the germs.

Droz likened the phenomenon to "objective tinnitus," the rare but unambiguous occurrence wherein a subject's ear-ringing will become amplified outwardly, so that others may actually hear the high-pitched tone, or the less common "gaze-tinnitus,"

Robert Hooke, *Bookworm* (1665).

wherein similarly "objective" pitches are produced by looking in a certain direction.

This being 1947, however, the localization movement of neurology had long since fallen into disrepute, never quite recovering from the pseudo-scientific fad of phrenology popular in the 19th century. Few were receptive to the idea that any one brain function could be circumscribed to any one area.

It can now be demonstrated through modern brain-imaging techniques, such as PET and fMRI, that not only are particular brain regions responsible for particular functions (notwithstanding a certain amount of neural plasticity), but that the brain is also a highly conductive engine whose cells communicate with each other through electrical pulses. It could very well be that neurons in the amygdala, the chief area accountable for the determination of danger, generate a common frequency perceivable by sympathetically "attuned" bacteria when stimulated by a real or imagined threat. Unfortunately—or perhaps very fortunately—none of this can be tested, as the disease was contained in 1948 and no metuspores are currently presumed to exist.

IV

It is impossible to know empirically, of course, whether a particular species has become extinct. We have no way of measuring with any degree of accuracy the breadth of microflora on Earth, never mind that which no longer exists. This becomes further complicated by the controversial notion that not all microorganisms are even, properly speaking, organisms.

The information age has familiarized us with figurative terms like "computer virus" and "artificial intelligence," but most of these are idioms meant to describe by way of analogy. To be sure, machines are neither sharp-witted nor capable of hosting biotic parasites. However, there is at least one species of bacteria whose constituent cells have been produced synthetically.

Pseudocytosporidium was engineered in the late '90s by a Korean bioterrorist group known as Bright Sun. The mechanical strain was not intended, like small pox or anthrax, to be distributed in subway cars or in well water as a means to cause massive damage and political upheaval, but rather to disrupt specific targets— those of other electrical engines.

Most bacteria are already, in a way, electrical. When they eat, they convert organic matter into carbon dioxide, releasing electrons, which are the currency of electrical power. *Pseudocytosporidia* were designed to metabolize in reverse, consuming electricity and converting it into kinetic energy, thereby annihilating whatever machinery they had been released into.

As for Bright Sun, their day appears to have set. No activity has been reported in recent years, and the group is thought to have disbanded. Whether or not their technology was leaked to other terrorist networks, however, remains anyone's guess.

V

Another bacterial oddity was reported to have flourished briefly in the marshy thickets of Southern India. Ensconced between Tishma Bay and the Port of Nadu lies a crescent-shaped plat of swampland known as the Sanchi-Khyim estuary, whose balmy climate and shallow, brackish waters provide an ideal breeding ground for microorganisms. One such species belonged to a class of bioluminescent protozoa known as *synccillia*, which has bedeviled researchers since its discovery.

It had long been rumored that late at night, through the dense tangle of rushes and bay reeds, local fishermen would sometimes spot a strange, multicolored fog pulsing from the mudflats. The Indian villagers believed it to be the result of departed ancestors writhing with jealousy at the living, but it was not until the invention of the microscope that the source of the vaporous strobe could be investigated scientifically.

Bioluminescence is the result of "cold light" emission, whereby the pigment luciferin is oxidized by the enzyme luciferase, producing a visible glow from within the organism. Millions of bioluminescent organisms exist, and their appeal has hardly diminished. *Phengodidae*, for instance, a family of glowing beetles, or the deadly "jack-o'-lantern" mushroom, whose gills dimly phosphorize in the dark, never cease to fascinate. The purpose of such an adaptation is multiform: some species use their self-generating light to attract mates, others use it defensively—for camouflage or to repulse predators—and still others use it to communicate. In the case of bacteria like *synccillia*, this last quality is referred to as "quorum sensing," meaning the ability of individual cells to coordinate actions within a group.

The only other organism known to bioluminesce synchronously is a rare species of tropical firefly found in the tidal waters of Malaysia, where swarms mysteriously flash in sync as they cluster about patches of mangroves.

This astonishing property has been of keen interest to scientists and mathematicians of late. The phenomenon of spontaneous order occurs throughout the natural world: biological systems like pacemaker cells in the heart that allow for a steady procession of beats; quantum structures like electrons that march in lockstep in a superconductor; water molecules that align themselves into crystalline form when the temperature has dropped below their freezing point.

Similarly, the pulses of *synccillia* result from what are known as coupled oscillators—systems linked in periodicity through chemical or physical means—the details of which are not yet fully understood. By whatever abstruse operating principle, these spores will blink in unison under certain conditions. It had been observed, for instance, that when infected, a host's organs would flash brightly from within like an X-ray, revealing the precise shape of the body's interior. Were it not for its alleged extinction, the *synccillus* cell might have been used for medical purposes, perhaps cloned and administered as a tracer—a luminous and living radiogram.

While these and other microorganisms—the most foreign and yet most furiously abundant creatures on the planet—continue to mystify us, it is to say nothing of that which we have not seen, those entombed in our undiscovered caverns or barnacled along the floors of the abyss or perhaps caked to the lining of your stomach. Our taxonomy will never be complete. Such is the diversity and complexity of this secret world that there seems to be little distinction between those of its inhabitants which truly exist and those which *may*.

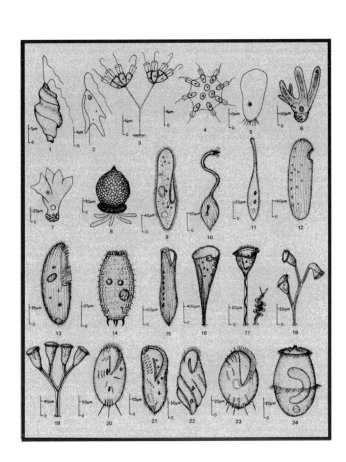

Those subway lines which travel briefly above ground take their passengers through

of sewing tables and thick silver ducts, gothic warehouses full of outdated electronica, a

buildings with dusty wooden floors and blacked-out windows, empty oil silos in the

But the city's secrets are not only a historical curiosity, they are equally a spectacle of

through apartments, craftsmen's studios, factories—places where living people live and work

hallways, pastry chefs mix and roll disks of fudge batter, couples make love, widowers

In a sense, the Library doesn't even stop there. In addition to exploring the material

inhabited by thoughts, delusions, memories . . .

arcane structures—vast supply depots, boarded up armories, abandoned mills with rows

decaying one-room schoolhouse, dilapidated foundries and assembly plants, condemned office

outskirts echoing raucously as the trains pass.

the unseen present. The same routes which expose the life of dead facilities move seamlessly

and sleep. Bakers knead the dough in their basement ovens, custodians mop the silent school

doze before glowing televisions.

world occupied by bodies and structures, it also seeks to penetrate the interior world—spaces

ENCHANTED LOOMS

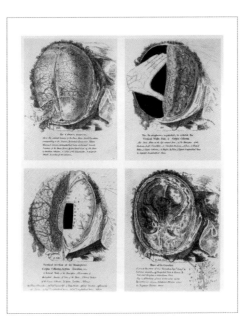

Neurological Anomalies

Alexander Ramsay, *Description of the Plates of the Brain* (1812). It was once believed that the brain and mind were separate entities—one a physical engine responsible for carrying out the involuntary tasks of the body; the other an antenna to the immaterial realm of thoughts and dreams. On closer inspection, however, these dual faculties appear to be a single system seen from two different perspectives.

INTRA-TEXTUAL CONFABULATION

The accident was sharp and sudden, like a thunderclap; the woman was propelled from her bicycle in a swift arc onto the pavement before her. Upon impact, her cranium split across the side, causing blood to stream into a fissure in her temporal lobe. She was rushed to an emergency room where she remained highly disoriented, having no recall of the crash.

The subject, DB, began displaying signs consistent with Korsakov's psychosis, a tragic condition characterized by severe amnesia coupled with anosognosia, a denial of the illness or impairment. What typically follows in such cases is a proliferation of confabulations concerning one's own identity and personal history. The subject fabricates a patchwork of fictions in order to mend the abrasions of memory and maintain a sense of narrative continuity. But occasionally there arise peculiar variations and complications, and specialists remain divided on whether or not to categorize them as separate phenomena altogether. DB was such an anomaly.

Rather than merely concocting a fictitious scenario to replace what she'd forgotten or obliterated, DB would requisition details, and often full scenes or plotlines, from fictional work she had read or viewed at some earlier point in her life. Fragments of soap operas, movies, romance novels, even long-buried children's

William Wegman, *Recreation* (2003). Oil and found postcards on three wooden panels. 84 x 144 x 2 inches (213.4 x 365.8 x 5 cm.) Courtesy Sperone Westwater, New York.

stories made an appearance in DB's ever-shifting account of her own life. She would routinely combine elements from one source with that of another, embellishing, say, the plotline of a courtroom drama with details from a television commercial.

In an article published by her attending physician, Dr. Sandeep Kumar, her mind was likened to a series of works by William Wegman, in which the artist had selected groups of similarly themed postcards and then painted "fake" landscapes to connect them, such that the full pieces appeared eerily, if lopsidedly, continuous.

Kumar went on to question whether there may have been a deeper truth being laced into the "confabulatory collage" DB was assembling. By enlisting a particular story, or by linking one source with another, was she attempting to communicate a veiled element of her own past?

While a number of psychologists found the notion plausible, most neuroscientists doubted the likelihood of such a possibility. However, it was later discovered by one Dr. Angelica Hayes, a cognitive neurologist at the Salk Institute, that fictional-historical transplacement systems like DB's may in some cases be reversed. When asked to recall a particular work of fiction they had been exposed to, a significant percentage of Hayes' subjects *imparted to the fictional work the missing or damaged elements from their own otherwise inaccessible memory*, apparently unaware that they had done so. From there it became possible for Hayes to reassemble shattered bits of inverted memories into continuous personal narratives.

It is of note that ITC is sometimes called "Pirandello Syndrome," referring to the author of *Six Characters in Search of an Author*, a play about a group of actors demanding that their own lives be dramatized by the playwright.

DYSANIMAGNOSIS

The "Uncanny" state described by Freud, wherein one believes inanimate objects such as dolls and wax figures possess life, finds its reciprocal delusion in Dysanimagnosis, the convinction that fellow human beings do not. Far from a hysterical belief, however, this phenomena finds its roots in direct and identifiable dysmorphisms of the brain.

Dysanimagnosis (from the Latin, *anima*, meaning "soul," and the Greek, *gnosis*, meaning "knowledge") is related to Capgras' Syndrome, the condition by which a subject will believe certain acquaintances to have been replaced with imposters or "doubles." But where Capgras' is generally limited to loved ones, people with an emotional connection to the subject, dysanimagnosis spares no one. All people, and even domestic animals such as dogs and cats, are believed by the subject to be robots or automata—lifeless engines carrying out pre-programmed tasks.

Both delusions often follow strokes of the hippocampus, one of the emotional centers of the brain, rendering subjects unable to access the nerve pathways that otherwise allow for empathy. With that connection severed, the subject is denied the sense of personal recognition that ordinarily accompanies human interaction, leaving her to conclude that as she herself feels nothing, the object providing the stimulus must not possess the requisite vitality necessary to generate a response. It is as if the subject is saying to herself, "the man who appears to be my husband couldn't possibly be him, because if he were, I would feel the corresponding affection—and I do not."

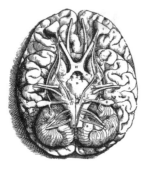

Vesalius, *View of the base of the brain with the optic chiasm at H* (1543).

Dysanimagnosis is presumed to operate on this framework, only to a far more drastic extent. Not only are parents and siblings exempt from a familial connection, but living beings on the whole are no longer convincing as animate organisms. Commonly, the subject will begin to believe that the world itself is a construction, that her surroundings are false, the buildings and trees merely set pieces in an elaborate façade designed to fool or test her.

Unlike schizophrenia, though, this paranoid condition often quells to a state of resignation and detachedness as she comes to "accept" her lot. She will likely start to develop a counter-identification, of sorts, wherein she applies to herself the mechanical properties she has bestowed to others, as if to say, "Since I, myself, feel nothing, then I too must be a machine." Following this, she extends this counter-identification to true machines, sometimes cultivating an interest in moving parts and simple motors, or at other times in games and puzzles. Just as certain types of fronto-temporal-dementia sufferers are occasionally known to develop sudden unforeseen interests in poetry or music, those afflicted with dysanimagnosis may become drawn with relentless absorption to riddles, mazes, codes and detective stories.

MNEMONIC CARTOGRAPHIA

It is common among hyper-mnemonics (those with photo-graphic memories) to use an imaginary "mapping" device as a means to retain information for indefinite periods of time. To wit: When a subject is presented with new information—relevant or otherwise—he may ensure its recall by plotting the mnemonic items within an imagined space such as a street or a house. This enables him to store any number of memories "topologically;" simply traveling through this environment mentally allows him to rediscover where he'd placed them. Far from being a pleasant utilitarian quirk, however, hyper-mnemosis is involuntary, and can be enormously disabling. Subjects are routinely incapacitated by an abundance of useless memories, and must therefore constantly wade through a muddle of detritus.

A different sort of crippling compulsion can be found in graphomaniacs, who are irresistibly determined to write, draw or scribble without any clear purpose—often resulting in feverishly composed strings of gibberish. Far more rare is a phenomenon which has been known to occur in subjects with bilateral lesions of the fronto-temporal cortex known as mnemonic cartographia. This curious affliction is functionally convergent in nature, binding hyper-mnemosis with graphomania through intra-modal paths.

The startling result is a subject who, rather than being paralyzed by eidetic recall, or incessantly compelled to scrawl graphemes, is surrounded by the mnemonic objects he'd placed about his environment. That is, every item that is committed to memory—a name, a price tag, a ticket confirmation number—is inscribed permanently into the landscape. Walking across the street in his home town, he is bombarded with a stream of letters, numbers, pictures; the train station is crowded with symbols and signs he'd mentally inscribed there; every temple in town has been graffitied with competing icons. The subject finds the artifacts of previous moments visually embedded into every surface. Almost invariably, he resolves to seek novel landscapes. But from this point on, his life is quick to degenerate into a breathless search for new maps, new cities, each adding to the ever-denser and more cluttered palimpsest of his world.

PROJECTIVE MULTIPLE PERSONALITY DISORDER

This phenomenon arises from a combination of two independent etiologies—one psychological, the other neurological—that overlap in a highly eccentric fashion. The first
condition, multiple personality disorder, is characterized by a
subject's assumption of various altered or split-off personalities
to which the host ego is oblivious. MPD is understood to be a
wholly mental illness, almost universally stemming from repressed
childhood trauma. The second condition, known as the Fregoli
Delusion, is marked by the monothematic conviction that different people are in fact the same person. The subject may attribute
any number of faces to a single personality whom he will often
suspect to be following or pursuing him. But unlike the former
delusion, this can be traced to specific loci of damage to "face-
recognition" nodes, located in the fusiform gyrus.

Simply put, Projective MPD is a nightmarish union of both
afflictions, whereby the ill-understood psychological matrices of
MPD may cross into the physiological realm by invading the
vacated nodal space.

Suddenly, the subject sustains the paranoid fantasy that his
own alters are populating the world around him. For instance, he
may encounter on the subway or the park any number of split-
off personae—a grade-school tormentor, an abusive parent, an

imaginary friend from childhood—unaware that he has conjured them from memory and projected them outwards. Astonishingly, however, when the subject is possessed of an altered persona, the characters may shift about him, and in fact he may encounter the *host* personality himself like a walking mirror.

SONOROUS NEGLECT

A disorder that has taken on many different names over the past century, sonorous neglect was first described in 1909 by R. D. Hicks, a student of the English neurologist, John Hughlings Jackson. Hicks observed a patient who claimed to be specifically and exclusively unable to perceive the music of Chopin.

The man, whom he called, simply, "J," betrayed no outward signs of madness. He was fully cognizant and perfectly functioning, able to perform his work, support his family and behave in an orderly, civil manner. Stranger still, there appeared to be nothing *physically* wrong with him either—no neuralgic dysfunction, no history of disequilibrium, not even any trace of hearing loss.

Hicks himself remained skeptical of the man's condition until he'd treated a different patient four years later, a woman suffering from epilepsy. Her seizures, he found, were dependably triggered by the sound of wind chimes—something about the timbre and pitch of clanging brass pipes (it was never discovered what) sent her immediately into convulsions. So-called "musicogenic epilepsy," as it was later termed, was a condition that had been described, though rarely in much detail, by physicians and philosophers since ancient times. Just as flickering photostrobic effects may elicit seizures in certain epileptics, others are susceptible to auditory stimuli, usually to vibrato or slewing, though occasionally to music.

When Hicks observed this baffling case, he thought of his earlier patient, J, and promptly began a new series of tests. He soon discovered that J was not "deaf" to all the music of Chopin, but curiously, only to the mazurkas. The Polish dance form itself, a vaguely rubato, off-kilter waltz with a displaced downbeat, when cradled by the fanciful drift of Chopin's melodies, provoked a corresponding astigmatism in the nervous system. This excitory interference effectively blocked the signal from the auditory cortex, vetoing the would-be perception of the offending sound.

Hicks' findings, which he described for the *Westminster Journal of Medicine* that February, was itself neglected. 1914 was the pivotal year for Freud's mounting celebrity, and psychoanalysis had begun to trump all other developments in psychology. Nearly all disorders of the brain, including epilepsy and autism, were quickly written off as disorders of

Hildegard von Bingen, *Liber Divinorum Operum* (13th century). A visionary artist, poet and musician, the Sybil of the Rhine, as she was sometimes called, is now believed by neurologists to have suffered from either migraine or migrainous epilepsy. The kaleidoscopic zigzags and vibrant coruscations in her work are characteristic of the aura states subjects often experience in the moments preceding seizures or attacks.

the *mind*—that is, as breeds of hysteria. The condition of "sonorous neglect" observed by Hicks was replaced by the term "selective timpanitis," and again by the overtly Freudian "hysterical deafness." The reasoning at that time was that, just as certain subjects may become psychosomatically blind under great stress, others may unconsciously *will* themselves into amusia. The culprit, it was claimed, lay in the clenched hands of that behemoth of Freudian theory, the narcissistic mother.

The tide turned once more, however, after the death of J in 1958. An autopsy was performed by the doctor's son, Edmund Hicks, who was eager to vindicate his father's name. What the young neurosurgeon found upon peeling back the layers of cranial tissue was a small hematoma lodged in the left superior temporal gyrus—one of the central nodes of rhythmic audition. Unfortunately, the paper, which was published by the *Journal of Clinical Neuropsychology* in 1961, was never corroborated by any follow-up studies, and the condition has remained largely unheard of ever since.

Another striking feature of the Library is the way it will seem to feature the very act of scure galleries and artists' lofts, themselves peculiar spaces with equally peculiar displays.

You will travel through rooms whose furniture is composed entirely of holograms, wallpaper patterns are framed while paintings, photographs, posters and calendars form the three-dimensional shadows, a cabinet of tiny scrolls, life-sized doll houses—places both

Finally, you'll find yourself in a museum exhibition. Viewers can be seen milling about, departs into the black tunnel that you realize that you yourself, your image in a subway

Perhaps the most ambitious exhibits, however, concern not presentation so much as presentation itself. If you stay on any train long enough, you will pass through a series of ob-

moving and vanishing in tandem with your gaze; one room is inverted, such that the

walls. Continue further and you will come upon increasingly fantastical spaces—a room of

mythical and personal, as if snatched from a dream.

observing the art, talking quietly amongst themselves, and it is not until the train again

window, were the display.

perception—the very act of seeing . . .

PICTURE THIS

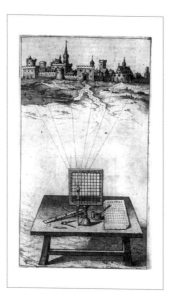

Lost Geographies, Impossible Topologies

Robert Fludd, *De Radiis Directis* (17th century). The depiction of the natural world has long remained a vexing challenge. If the Earth was a sphere in reality, why was it impossible to represent on a plane? Conversely, if certain functions of higher mathematics made sense on the page, why could they not be transposed to actual space?

PAPÔS

The best kept secrets of the Greeks were not the powerful maritime weapons devised by Archimedes, nor the mystical properties possessed by "golden" proportions, but the unnerving imperfections underlying both. These crude blotches of apparent nonsense were ignored by most mathematicians, but the more the field progressed, the more ill-tempered enigmas crept in.

For instance, a square was considered a perfect geometric object—all sides of equal length, four right angles uniting them harmoniously. But drawing a diagonal line between one corner and the opposite corner gave rise to trouble, for the ratio of that diagonal to the length of the side did not result in an even fraction, but a maddening spate of endless decimals.

So fretful was this observation to Pythagoras that he and his brotherhood chose to keep it from sight, militantly denying its existence to all outsiders. To speak of it at all was heresy. But irrational numbers were sprouting up with increasing frequency and it was becoming difficult to uphold the doctrine of numerical purity. When the unfortunate Hippasus of Metapontum threatened to reveal the secrets of π and the other irrationals, the Pythagoreans had the feisty geometer thrown from the deck of a ship.

Or so legend has it. Whatever the fate of Hippasus, rumors of his supposed demise made their way across the Grecian isles.

When they migrated toward Papôs, a small town north of Kavála, bordering on Geton (modern-day Bulgaria), they reached the ears of a nervous yet precocious architectural apprentice named Cretheus, who had recently made an unsettling discovery of his own. He'd discovered that, in order to represent a three-dimensional space on a two-dimensional plane, it was necessary to presume an infinitesimally small point to which all lines parallel to the viewer's sight must recede. Thus, to render objects the way they appeared to the eye, heretical concepts betraying the purity of numbers must be applied.

Peter Paul Rubens, Frontispiece to *Book V of Aguilonius* (1613).

Naturally, the consequence of disclosing such truths was not at all appealing to the young draftsman, and yet how could he deny the raw facts of perspective? He resolved to design buildings whose dimensions would prove impervious to optical foreshortening. Abandon depth and there would be no infinity to recede to.

The resulting drawings were proportionally distorted. Viewed from one perspective, the structures would appear flat, while from another they were isometric; yet from no particular angle would they seem to abide natural dimensions. If an entire city were built along anamorphic coordinates, he reasoned, the secret math could remain safely at bay.

Cretheus went to work on the model in his studio, a 20%-scale city of illusions, within which he would eat, sleep, draw and sculpt. He lived in this *trompe l'oeil* metropolis for weeks on end, expanding it, perfecting every angle and every curve. Awestruck servants would bring him mutton and berries, but often found their master too feverish with excitement to be hungry.

Still, the plan was fraught with complications. Shadows revealed depth, as did light—distant objects, he knew, appeared slightly blurry and bluer than closer ones, due to the atmosphere in between, not to mention the phenomenon of motion parallax. This last issue, the apparent shift in angular position of two or more objects relative to the observer's movement, proved especially difficult to overcome, as it was a direct by-product of binocular vision.

After several months of living in his model city, however, Cretheus awoke to find the problem suddenly and mysteriously alleviated. Buildings, temples, the stadium, the library—all appeared curiously hollow, compressed. His stereoscopy (the ability to perceive in three-dimensions) had gone, taking with it the memory of having existed at all. Shadows were not signifiers of occlusion but their own shapes, trapezoidal, parabolic, each a singular body. The vanishing points had vanished.

It was not until Cretheus finally left the miniature Papôs that he realized what had happened. Upon opening the doors to face the sun-dappled outside, he glimpsed a world he'd never before seen. Onion domes, which had previously appeared as flat ovals in the distance, now protruded in full, shimmering rotundity. Simple gardens were vertiginous swaths of color and shade, extending far into the distance. Structures which obscured others seemed holographically projected from their backgrounds. The world was—for a brief time—a dynamic weave of focal relationships, each distance a marvelous and delicate thread. It was as if the ontology of space itself, not only his sense of geospatial orientation, had been transfigured.

It is not known whether Cretheus remained in the macroscopic world with its impure ratios or returned to the hygienic, orderly one of his own construction. What is known is that he demonstrated that it is indeed possible to eradicate the heathen numbers embedded in our visual universe—so long as the mind is fit to create its own.

CITY OF INFINITE BRIDGES

Mathematicians may be familiar with the stories of Königsberg, city of seven bridges, but few are aware—and even fewer convinced—of the startling events surrounding them.

The former capital of East Prussia, Königsberg (now Kaliningrad, Russia) is remembered chiefly for the famous math problem solved by Leonhard Euler in the 18th century. The city contained two islands enclosed by the river Preger, each connected to the mainland and to one another by seven bridges. The puzzling question submitted by Euler was whether all seven bridges could be crossed in a single trip without doubling back.

Anon., Map of Königsberg (1807).

In a feat of public curiosity that seems almost inconceivable by modern standards, the townspeople began to walk about on

Sundays trying to solve the problem themselves. Of course, no one could, and in fact Euler proved that such a quest was impossible.

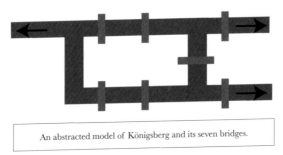

An abstracted model of Königsberg and its seven bridges.

The mathematician's wife, Katharina Gsell, was known to dabble in numbers herself, but her own contributions have for the most part been written off as the whimsical diversions of a Swiss housewife. Her gifts have only recently come to light due to the fortuitous discovery of her half-sister's diary, into which a very strange sketch had been inscribed. It is of note that Euler eventually left Katharina for this very same sister, and that the geometrical figure was composed as a spiteful refutation of her ex-husband's celebrated proof.

The diagram was not of the sort Euler had drafted—in fact, it is likely no one had ever conceived such a configuration. It was essentially a map of Königsberg plotted on a familiar Cartesian grid, only folded to link two of its corners as if by an adhesive. The resulting shape—something of an inward-facing loop— allowed the connected landforms to function as a single "node," thereby off-setting the numbers in Euler's math. In this tangled, imaginary city, all seven bridges could be traversed in a single, non-repeating route.

Katharina's visionary graph presaged the science of elliptical geometry and would almost certainly have inaugurated this revolutionary field (just as her ex-husband's work had helped establish topology) had her ideas ever been taken seriously. This being 18th-century Europe, few believed feminine minds capable of rational thought, let alone complex mathematics, and this lack of validation further incensed her. Katharina grew feverish with rage. She barely ate, stopped sleeping almost completely, and channeled all her fury into the city that had caused her such torment.

Shortly thereafter, reports of bizarre happenings began to surface. Townspeople spoke of having dreadful dreams, visions of natural disaster—floods, earthquakes, hurricanes—which ravaged the city night after tempestuous night. The collective despair soon carried into the waking hours, and for many there was no respite at all. Some wept, others went into self-exile, a few even threw themselves from the town's now-famous bridges.

To this day, it is believed by certain citizens of Kaliningrad that Katharina's proof was a curse upon the town, that it brought their ancestors to the brink of madness, and that it was not until Euler and his two wives had died that the plague of nightmares was lifted.

GOLIIJO

Another disquieting riddle was proposed by the mathematician Benoît Mandelbrot, who in 1967 raised the seemingly innocuous question, "How long is the coastline of Britain?" What he found was startling: that the smaller the increments of measurement, the longer the measured length became. For instance, if one was to lie a yardstick over a large map of Britain—or any coastline—one would get a particular measurement, say, 6 inches. Yet if he were to use a small ruler with finer increments he would find, impossibly, that the length was now slightly larger, say, 6.01 inches. Reducing the measuring stick still further would yield ever-increasing lengths—6.015, then 6.0157, then 6.01579—and so on, without end. This observation spawned the science of fractals, the mysterious broken dimensions that lay *between* whole numbers.

Few realize, however, that fractal dimensions are more than just theoretical constructs. A case in point is the city of Goliijo, an island city-state that has flummoxed geometers and travelers alike throughout its existence. No matter which direction the traveler approaches Goliijo from, the landscape is the same—an etched bank of lichen-rich clefts flanked by two great shelves of rock, each with a thousand outstretched fingers. On arrival, he comes upon a spattering of zinc-roofed houses and narrow, canal-combed streets, where merchants sell silver-scaled fish and red bell peppers. A funeral procession leads up a cobblestone path toward the golden-spired cathedral. Near the center of town sits the forum, a wide structure of polished limestone, inside which villagers shop at small bakeries and a portly senator orates at the rostrum.

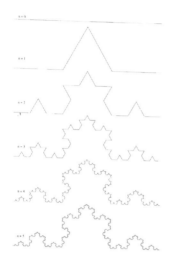

The first five iterations of the Koch Curve, whose finite area is paradoxically enclosed within an infinite perimeter.

However, something curious befalls the traveler once he passes the busy central market with its wide cement colonnades. At every intersection, it seems, the paths subdivide into others, each a mirror image of the last, and in two or three more turns he finds himself hopelessly lost.

For the inhabitants of Goliijo, however, there is no such thing as lost, no such concept. There is no need for maps because the city is itself a map. Every detail of Goliijo is an inscription of its own layout. A single iteration of a leaf matches the shape of the full tree. Viewing Goliijo's coastline from a satellite reveals the same image as one of its grains of sand under a microscope. Everywhere is home. Every child is one's own.

If the traveler stays long enough, he too will become inscribed into its landscape; he will be absorbed into its history, its future— "lostness" itself will be lost.

The only way for a traveler to escape is to have brought a spool of twine with which to trace his route back like Ariadne.

WALDEMAR

For years, travelers have tried in vain to discover the city of Waldemar. Like Atlantis, the little evidence of its existence has become shrouded by wishful dreams and legend. Unlike Atlantis, however, its myth concerns not the past but potential futures.

Waldemar is said to be an entire city enclosed within a single castle. A serpentine rivulet circumscribes the land like a moat, only there is no drawbridge—the sustainable city reaps what it requires from within its walls and incinerates its refuse through a giant, open-faced tower. There are also no windows, no parapets, no indicators of a world beyond, and for its inhabitants, no such world exists.

What Waldemar does have is rooms. The castle-city is believed to house countless chambers of countless variety—some, plush drawing rooms thick with pipesmoke; others, fetid, yellow-tiled cells sponged with mold—and more are added each day. The vast network is something of a maze of cubes, each holding a series of possibilities. Choosing one door over another, a citizen may find himself in a long, cedar-wood wardrobe draped with hundreds of furs and linens, a hot, narrow kitchen pungent with the smell of pig's blood, a bathhouse, an oubliette. He may stay as long as he likes in any given room but there is no way to predict whether the next will be more or less suitable to him. Further troubling is that there is no turning back, for each door can only be opened from one side.

In Waldemar, time and destiny are a literal function of the combination of entrances and exits one has chosen. The city's architecture forms and reforms itself in proportion to the paths taken by each of its inhabitants—or perhaps the more appropriate term is "tenants," as each space is occupied only until the next choice has been made. In this sense, Waldemar may be thought of as a kind of living hotel.

What happens when two or more people occupy the same room? This scenario presents itself all the time and may result in any number of outcomes—a deadly brawl to gain ownership, an amicable settlement, a lustful tryst, a mutual departure, a simple, forgettable dialogue, or, rarely, a symbiotic cohabitation.

What if two people fall in love with one another but not with the space? This presents yet another problem: the lovers must choose either to resign themselves to fate and cut their losses, or to go their separate ways hoping to cross paths in the future. One thing they may not do is leave through the same door.

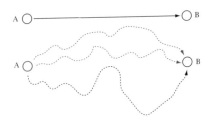

Multiple histories: three possible electron paths with a common destination.

Particle physicists have likened Waldemar to the "multiple histories" model proposed by Richard Feynman, wherein the universe is continuously branching into divergent copies of itself as each possible electron orbit is realized.

Others claim the city is more akin to a massive brain—a lattice of criss-crossing paths and states whose very armature shifts in response to the information it receives.

Yet another theory is that every inhabitant of the city is a different permutation of the same character who has merely made different choices. Perhaps this is why no traveler may discover it: he has been there all along.

The Library's exhibits are not always visual. There are places underground where the

by chains of small fluorescent bulbs. The whirring engine is cut, the windows are slid open,

like the imprisoned breath of an ancient pyramid. And slowly, quietly, the music becomes

Of course, it is not music as it's traditionally understood to be, but rather the result of

dome-like chamber, where the tones reverberate and repel and split and regroup into

with the buzz of electric currents oscillating across copper cables; the jittery clanks of suction

it is overpowering, deafening—its beauty otherworldly, the sonorous equivalent of a black

the windows are promptly sealed, the lights return, and the train sets back on its course to

train will simply stop unannounced and the lights will fade to reveal a cavernous recess lit

and in moments the reader is turned into a listener. A warm, moist air swells into the car

audible.

countless pipes and grids which span the circumference of the city emptying into one vacant,

ever-shifting harmonies—cylinders of oil sloshing through narrow tin arteries mingle

pumps measure rhythms in the whistling wind tunnels—a symphony of infrastructure. Soon

hole or a supernova. It is at this moment, this strange awakening to a world of sound, that

the final exhibition . . .

THE MUSICAL ILLUSIONIST

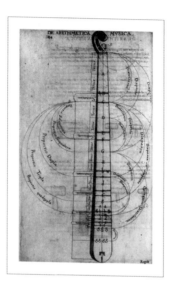

The Life and Times of Phelix Lamark

Robert Fludd, *De Arithmetica Musica* (1617). A polymath with mystic inclinations, Fludd was deeply influenced by the syncretistic philosophy
of Pythagoras, particularly the mathematician's notion that harmonic
intervals corresponded to the mechanics of the cosmos. Both believed
that the celestial bodies emitted tones to which the human ear had
grown too accustomed to perceive.

I

The world repaginates; every so often, human concerns either crystallize, taking shape and developing order, or vanish into obscurity.

In the 19th century, science struggled to disentangle itself from the knotted loom of curiosities it had been in times past. The great movement toward specialization, quantification and precision of measurement that had begun in the Renaissance swelled to its apex during the Industrial Revolution. Alchemists, unrelenting in their pursuit of elemental properties, drifted from mere charlatans bent on curing gold from copper. Numerologists, more assiduous in their study of mathematical patterns and systems than in decoding ancient prophecies, found themselves in universities rather than abbeys. Naturalists, content to explain disease as the result of corrupted "essences," continued to treat patients with leeches and prayer, while those who persisted in developing a theoretical framework for germs became physicians. The natural was becoming cleaved from the supernatural.

The art world underwent a similar departure. Painters ceased to depict solely religious symbology and royalty, opening up to the more immediate and tangible world of natural scenes—landscapes free of scriptural relevance: peasant workers, nudes, everyday objects. Musicians were emancipated from liturgical texts and hymns, free to experiment with alternative forms outside the Church and high court. Art, like science, diverged from spiritual influence.

During this dramatic galvanization—or erosion, depending on one's perspective—were a number of noted figures who rejected these dissolutions. To them, physics was inextricable from metaphysics, as was painting from optics and ethics from politics; integration, they argued, was a necessary attribute of scholarship without which progress was inconceivable.

Among this dissenting minority was Étienne-Jules Marey, the French physiologist whose chronophotographic studies of animal locomotion influenced both Edison and the Lumiere brothers, helping spawn the industry of cinema; Goethe, the German playwright whose theories of color perception appended those of Newton; Hermann Helmholtz, the prolific physicist-cum-psychologist; and the now all-but-forgotten Welch inventor, Phelix Lamark.

II

Born in a small district in Flintshire around 1830, Lamark was raised by a provincial anatomist named Frederick. Scarcely anything is known about the family's early years other than their eventual exile from Britannia for Frederick's "inhumane" practice of vivisection—experiments on live animals—a method revolutionary for the life sciences elsewhere in Europe. Ostracized from his "beast-loving" community and threatened with legal action, Lamark Sr. took wife and child and fled south to Paris where he became an adjunct professor of medicine at the *Collège de France*. It was here in the plush libraries and ornate laboratories that the young Phelix caught his first glimpse of the scientific world.

Before an ample audience of medical students and lay spectators, his father would perform his demonstrations in a smallish indoor amphitheater, and Phelix would delight in the surgical presentations. Something about the space, the dimly lit seats slanting toward the bright stage, the rows of strange implements lining the walls like props backstage at an opera house—slender vials and jars of opaque glass, zinc scissors and steel saws, electrical conduction machines boxed in polished oak, meters and dials of every shape and size, translucent tubes, straws, needles—seemed mystical and otherworldly. Here germinated in Phelix's mind the infusion of science with theater, illumination with fantasy.

Without question, Mrs. Lamark was key in augmenting this fascination. As was common for women in bourgeois society, she would entertain the family in the evenings with her piano playing. Additionally, Mrs. Lamark patiently instructed her son each morning on the fundamentals of fingering and harmony, which helped to transpose his wonder from the visual modality to the audible.

Much to her chagrin, Phelix would play tricks on her by detuning the strings. Some nights his manipulations were subtle, such as tweaking two adjacent notes the same pitch, while on others—depending on his mood—he was more ambitious, reformatting the entire keyboard by mere quarter tones off. He was so tickled by the howl and sting of such nebulous sonorities that in his early teens, he constructed a fourth pedal that shifted the pitches up and down by fractions of a semitone when pressed.

Friends later recalled other musical pranks the boy would conduct in the household, such as shaving slices off the porch wind chimes to create disturbingly dissonant rings, or scattering bottles of varying heights and densities in different rooms, so that when a strong breeze rose up, the house seemed to cry like a widow in mourning.

III

Why certain sounds were pleasant to the ear and others unpleasant was a subject of inexhaustible interest to Lamark. It was clear to him from an early age that the human body, like the goats and dogs his father so carefully disassembled, was a complex machine crafted by nature. Why should it respond with such deep repulsion to certain frequencies and amplitudes and with rapture to others?

Of equal concern were the many similarities between the human body and the structure

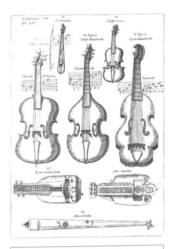

Athanasius Kircher, *Figura Chelys Hexachorda*, from *Musurgia Universalis* (1650).

of musical instruments—indeed, both consisted of a skeleton of sorts, upon which valves, threads, pumps, pipes and casings operated harmoniously for the purpose of exerting pressures and distributing materials. Was there an innate connection between a man's auditory system and a man-made plate strung with vibrating cables? What could account for the mysterious sonic alchemy that crossed the æther from soundboard to eardrum? Somewhere between acoustical physics and human physiology—between flesh and spirit—lay the answer.

Lamark approached this problem from a mechanical angle. Apprenticed to the celebrated Italian craftsman Federico Pontito, he repaired a wide array of damaged instruments, from strings

126

and percussion to woodwinds and brass, for the better part of a decade. Lamark especially enjoyed working with musical trinkets and toys such as music boxes and player pianos, and was said to have treated the elements of acoustical craftwork—hitch pins, tension rods, cabinetry, steel fiber—with the gentle care he would have a human body.

The analogy proved more than figurative as he eventually left the repair shop to enroll in medical school. This, too, resulted in a dead end; Lamark was expelled after less than a year for having taken "indecent liberties" with his work. One night he was caught by a custodian attempting to install an accordion-like voice box into the throat of a cadaver. After Lamark's termination many more of his experiments were discovered, such as limb prostheses, inner organs replaced with various polymer materials and a corpse whose shoulder blades had been rigged to a large pair of mechanical wings.

At this point Lamark seems to have disappeared for several years. It is said that he took on various odd jobs—a photographer's assistant, a carriage driver, a traveling insurance salesman, a children's tutor and an occasional translator of Dutch epics. He emerged in the early 1860s having received word of Clerk Maxwell's famous experiment with color projections. Essentially, what Maxwell had done was backlight three black-and-white slides of the same object onto a screen simultaneously, each with a lantern tinted

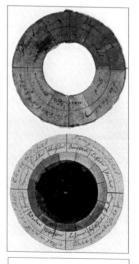

Johann Wolfgang Goethe, *Rose of the Humors* (1799).

127

a different primary color. When the three filtered projections—
one green, one red, one violet—were lined up correctly, a magnificent full color image leapt off the screen. The resulting conclusion was that the human eye worked in much the same manner as the layered filtrations. Different photoreceptors were "tuned" to receive light from these equivalent primary colors, out of which an endless spectrum could be constructed in the brain. This replaced the existing theory that retinal cells were somehow innately receptive to an infinite band of wavelengths.

These new findings naturally rekindled Lamark's curiosity about the mechanics of the senses, particularly audition, which had been a preoccupation of his since childhood. What gave rise to consonance and dissonance in the aural cavity? Did the ear take "vibrational snapshots" to be set in motion by the temporal cortex? Where did *noise* end and *music* begin?

Now a striking gentleman in his mid-30s—tall, gaunt and somewhat pale-skinned, with a high forehead and sea-green eyes—he set out to begin his own research.

After a long and discouraging quest for a benefactor, Lamark was discovered rather serendipitously by one Samson Peterdi, a sly, Hungarian industrialist with an eye for off-beat innovation. The two met in a Parisian bistro late one night—an ambitious but desperate engineer with nothing to his name and a portly, divorced financier twice his age. They struck up an amicable conversation about their mutual disenchantment with contemporary opera, its incessant fads and empty sentiment, until the elder made an off-kilter remark about German composers apparently so rousing to the younger that Lamark challenged him to a duel. Perhaps it was the absinthe they were drinking, but upon seeing the furious sparkle in his eyes, Peterdi believed he'd found in Lamark the boisterous youthful spirit he'd been searching for, and more or less immediately agreed to underwrite all of his future work.

IV

Elysium Laboratories, the brainchild of Lamark and Peterdi, was inaugurated in the spring of 1864. The building was converted from a dilapidated storehouse in the old section of Montmartre into a full-service production and development studio. With a high-ceilinged shop in back and a 250-odd seat oratorium in front, the space was perfectly suited for the manufacture and demonstration of Lamark's prolific output of devices, experiments and ideas.

Unlike the ornate furnishings of the *Collège de France*, however, Elysium was crude in its accommodations. Creaky, wooden chairs sat on cold stone floors, sparsely covered by worn and porous throw rugs. There were no rooms as such; the many partitions had become so moldy that Lamark chose to tear down all but the bearing walls, leaving the cross beams and plumbing chase exposed. The remaining dividers held tarnished, gilt-framed mirrors, large anatomical diagrams and faded mechanical schematics. It is perhaps not surprising that most visitors were initially put off.

V

Lamark's first exhibition was advertised in *La Lune* as "An Evening of Musical Phantasmagoria," and drew some seventy-five viewers. The show began with a performance of Haydn's *String Quartet in D Major*. By all accounts, the first movement was played flawlessly, the violinists' bowing tapered to a subtle caress to counteract the harsh acoustics. During the second movement, though, certain members of the audience succumbed to a sudden wooziness. Something queer was afoot; some claimed it was a rise in temperature while others mentioned a foul odor. Slowly, it became clear that the strangeness had to do with the music itself, which seemed to emanate not only from the stage but from the anterior wall—it was coming from behind them while the musicians clearly performed straight ahead. As the piece went on, in fact, the music appeared to shift direction like the wind—at one point, from above, from another, below—ever so gradually receding and protracting about the hall.

Many speculated that there was a second quartet traveling back behind the entrance and up above the gaslight grid, though it wasn't clear how the musicians could have possibly moved so quickly, nor made the slightest noise as they raced from one position to another.

One critic compared the experience to a kind of musical daguerreotype or ambrotype. Just as a two-dimensional plate contains a continuity of perspective, he argued, so Lamark's "phantasmagoria" represented a study in "aural dimensionality." Depth, focus and distortion were treated as malleable attributes in musical space.

Not all the reviews were favorable. Another critic, one Marcel D'Aubigne, of the conservative *L'Informateur* dismissed Lamark's project as a "damnable offense, epitomizing the shameless emphasis our musicians and music-composers have placed upon gimmickry and adolescent frivolity." Unaffected, Lamark went to work on his next production, *Study in Fracture No. 2*.

This controversial work seemed to have no concrete beginning, much like the dotted demarcations on old maps where the boundaries between adjoining states remained undecided. Rather, as the gas lamps dimmed, one simply became more aware of the various creaks and whispers of the theater itself. Wind sifted through cracks and doorways, latecomers shuffled to their seats. Elderly couples adjusted their monocles, children tapped their feet while the stage remained bare. Some sniffled or shifted in anticipation. The muffled clapping of hooves on cobblestone could be heard intermittently from outdoors. Windowpanes rattled. Finally, an unseen consonance began to transfigure from the relative silence, a kind of "primordial gloam," as one audience member put it. A purring open fourth resounded through the hall, as though an invisible orchestra had arisen from the audience. Was this an ironic reference to the cosmogonic majesty of Germanic preludes? Was it to demonstrate that raw sound itself was as celestial as music? Or merely to navigate that inchoate no-man's-land between order and chaos? It remains unclear.

Throughout the piece, extra-musical elements prattled about an unwavering network of central harmonies—clawing, scraping; strange mews and breys—at times almost imperceptibly quiet, at others, searingly cacophonous, until about forty minutes later, the strings and bells subsided, leaving a ghost of sonorous color hovering in the form of breathy murmurs, toneless plucks and gently thumping dampers.

Those patient enough to stay through the whole performance either found it transcendent or vile; few fell in between. This is not to suggest that the former deemed it *musically* important. None of Lamark's creations were meant to belong in any canon or repertoire, as they were one-of-a-kind events. Rather, those receptive to the stagings simply found the experience pleasant, either for its puzzling ambiguity or its dreamlike otherness. They may not have known what it was or even what to call it—a scientific demonstration? a musical event? a magic show?—but the very unclassifiability of *Fracture* may have been what intrigued viewers to attend Lamark's next event.

Meanwhile, Lamark had become heavily invested in the work of geometers Bernhard Riemann and János Boylai, who were helping to ferment a new form of mathematics that refuted some of the postulates of Euclid. So-called "non-Euclidean" geometry described a new set of rules that emerged when one applied "flat" geometric principles to hyperbolic or elliptical figures. For instance, it was observed that two infinitely long parallel lines—previously thought to remain parallel, by definition, forever—would actually deviate or *meet* on a spheri-cal manifold. In other words, many of the accepted axioms about space and dimensional-ity had to be reconsidered or subsumed by new ones.

Could there be a revolu-tion in Pythagorean harmony as there had been in Euclid-ean geometry? The question was so electrifying to Lamark that he set out to experiment with curvatures in *sonic* space.

Drawing from the findings of Christian Doppler, who'd first described the physics of frequency variation relative to moving media two decades earlier, Lamark designed a "kinetic symphony" unique

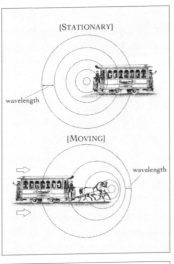

The Doppler Effect. The pitch of a sound varies according to the speed at which the observer and/or the source is moving relative to one another. A train whistle, for instance, appears to rise in pitch as the caboose approaches the station and dimin-ish as it departs, because the constituent wavelengths are foreshortened or elongated relative to the observer.

to the architecture of the Elysium Theater. The new staging was the first of Lamark's to sell out, and from the many accounts subsequently published, we shall attempt to reconstruct the experience.

As the audience shuffled into the auditorium, the piece had already begun. The lights were up and the twenty-two-piece orchestra was seated at the stage performing an unrecognizable *allegro*. No one in the crowd seemed to be quite sure whether they had arrived so late that they'd missed the beginning or so early that the orchestra was still rehearsing. In any case, the uncertainty set a highly uncomfortable tone. Once the chattering and shooshing settled, certain few audience members noticed a slightly distracting echo, and as the symphony progressed, the echo became more and more pronounced. It was as if the piece were somehow growing in resonance, the delay incrementally increasing with each phrase. Was the air in the theater growing denser, more humid? Were reflective materials being slipped surreptitiously into the space? One listener went as far as to wonder if the ceiling was an optical illusion concealing a dome with removable horizontal partitions. Another questioned whether the orchestra was even performing live music, or if there was a hidden machine somehow transmitting music from another location, like a telegraph.

As the symphony grew distantly out-of-phase with itself, other curious happenings began to arise. The echoes were now so displaced that they seemed to carry their own unique character and rhythm. Were they in fact overtaking their source? Not only were the echoes apparently rising in volume, they were also falling out of key. Fractional pitches were washing back like tonal shadows, elongated and curved. The shifts became their own reverberations, their own waveform, and it soon became impossible to tell which phase was the clone.

Conflicting interpretations abounded. Was this intended as a mockery of Europe's reverance for symphonic form? An inspired experiment in style? An acoustical hall of mirrors? Or was it a deeply misguided exercise in temperament? Some even wondered if Lamark was deaf. All these questions remained maddeningly unresolved. Peterdi, who rarely commented on his beneficiary's progress, described the new work as a "symphony within a symphony; each embedded or inscribed between the notes of the other."

Still, this did not explain or account for the distended pitches, the curious mesh of microtonal harmonies that seemed to slide vertiginously back and forth from the orchestra. Perhaps the most interesting theory came from an engineer who believed the entire theater to be mobile, spinning centripetally on its axis and creating inversions from diminishing and expanding Doppler waves. But, needless to say, this would have required a complete structural overhaul of the original building, a feat of which there remains no evidence.

VI

Lamark and his "musical illusions" were now established in the thoroughfare, fast becoming a hot topic of debate among society folk. Strangely, it was the elite class, comprised mostly of artists and scientists, who found Lamark's work most disquieting. While both groups were dividing and subdividing—painters fanning into ever-more specific schools, each armed with an exclusive manifesto; natural philosophers into cosmologists, cell biologists, mathematical physicists and so forth—Elysium sought the very opposite, a synthesis of disciplines, a conviction which infuriated nearly everyone.

In response to a typically inflammatory editorial in *L'Informateur*, Lamark defended his work as a necessary antidote to the ever-forking paths of modern scholarship. "Specialization," he wrote, "can only lead to further specialization—and to what end? . . . Human endeavors will become as fractured as the stars, isolated and scattered, with no constellation to hold them in place." He likened "academic fortification" to a labyrinth from which there was no return. "Innovation without cross-pollination is an absurdity; without *integrated* research there can no breadth of imagination. Need I remind Monsieur d'Aubigne that Rome met its fate not by falling siege to outsiders, but by slowly fragmenting from the inside?"

D'Aubigne was not impressed. "Are we to believe," he retorted venomously, "that Lamark's tomfoolery holds the skeleton key to future discovery? That he alone, by inducing nausea with his interminable barnyard squawks and deafening cowls, is truly ushering forth an age of intellectual enlightenment as he so claims?"

In a letter to the editor published the following week, Lamark wrote, "[I]t is coming to light that all the imponderables—heat, electricity, magnetism—are manifestations of the same force. This insight would not have been possible without a groundwork of common principles. It is conceivable that many other fundamental energies, such as gravity and impetus, may too prove to be properties linked by an ecumenical potential, as Aristotle foresaw. The infinite divisions we have erected in our quest for knowledge are but false categories obstructing the true nature of that which is."

D'Aubigne remained staunchly unconvinced and continued to lambaste Lamark and everything associated with Elysium Laboratories.

VII

By the early 1870s, Lamark had inspired an intimate band of followers who not only devoutly attended each performance at Elysium, but sought to carry on the tradition of "Musical Illusionism" themselves. André Bazin, a noted young industrial designer, staged his *Symphonie Méchanique* in an abandoned coal processing plant just north of Paris. Instead of employing the use of musicians or instruments at all, Bazin was said to have released hundreds of mechanical butterflies into the space, each tuned to a different pitch. The result was an enveloping tide of harmonies that swept, buzzing and humming, through the stuffy air for several minutes before fluttering out a portal in the ceiling.

Another Illusionist show, realized by the former gallery curator Jacques Tatou, featured a room full of "magical boxes" with which individual viewers could interact. Among these small receptacles of wonder were sea shells said to actually reproduce the sound of the ocean, complete with crashing waves and crying gulls. At least two witnesses claimed to hear faint calliope music when listening intently through the crevice. Some denied that anything was audible at all—that Tatou was simply using a form of "suggestion" to induce the appearance of organized tones. Others guessed that he had inserted a small band of iron that received a radio signal from a transmitter hidden nearby, while others still believed Tatou's spirit had been imbued with "dark energies"—a claim he was loathe to deny.

Rumors began to spread that these men and several others were not imitators of Lamark but *conduits* of his own designs, hands that Lamark had hired as a means to demonstrate his own influence, when in fact it was he who had secretly created each new illusion. The Council on Public Art and Decency Standards threatened to file suit under the Fraudulence Act, but there appeared to be no law against crediting others with work that was actually one's own, unless the work itself violated the law, so the suit was retracted.

That summer, Lamark suffered a stroke. He was treated for just over two months at the Salpêtrière Hospital and released that fall. Friends noted a distinct change in temperament. Whereas he was once jocular and mischievous, he was now soft spoken, even saturnine. Lamark retreated into his work, made fewer and fewer public appearances. There is no record of his having participated in any further discourse; there are no publications to speak of, nor any letters or correspondences.

The surviving notebooks from this period, however, are nearly blackened with ink. The small bit that remains legible seems to be concerned with the then-highly mysterious phenomenon of synaesthesia, or "colored-hearing." Glued to one particularly dense page of jottings and sketchings was a small article from a medical journal concerning the neurological origins of the experience. We may infer from this that despite Lamark's prolonged silence and debilitated state, his mind was as active as ever.

Whether there was any physiological correlation between his stroke and his interest in synaesthesia remains a subject of some debate. We find in one notebook a chart detailing a spectrum of color-coded musical pitches. The key of $C^{#}$, for example, was linked to the color of "vulcanized rubber." A^{b} corresponded to "vermillion red;" F, to "eggplant;" $D^{#}$, to "cobalt." Written in the margin next to the color dial is a gradient bar, perhaps suggesting that each color grew fainter or less vibrant as the pitches

rose. Was he being casually metaphoric, like the contemporane-
ous poet Rimbeau, or did he experience a true cross-wiring of
the senses? Whatever the reason for Lamark's sudden preoccupation, it culminated in the final stage piece of his career.

Largely regarded as his seminal work, *Chromatica* did away
with musical performance altogether—or so it seemed. As the
audience took their seats on the evening of July 11th, 1873, the
lights suddenly clamped off, leaving the space in pitch blackness.
People gasped, several shrieked. The curtain then lifted to reveal
nothing but a luminously white canvas stretched from floor to
ceiling. A dull straw-colored glow faded up, slowly swallowing the
white in its amber yolk, only to recede into a graduated shadow.
From this, a pale indigo began to bleed, shivering into streaks
of milky green. The direction of the light sources was not at all
evident; perhaps there was only one lamp from behind, upon
which differently colored veils were being drawn, but this would
not explain the light's peculiar dynamism, its languid swells and
dissolves. Whatever the case may have been, the audience sat
entranced by the successively melting colors before them.

At this point in the show, however, a second and far more
arresting phenomenon took place, though accounts differ greatly.
One reporter noted an abrasive timpanic *bang* while another dis-
tinctly recalled the soft plucking of harp strings. Even dour Samson Peterdi described in his personal journal being struck by the
"kaleidoscopic swath of distant church bells."

It did not end there. People recorded categorically incom-
patible accounts of the same event—trenchant marching drums,
biting piccolo jabs, whispering string glissandos, hoarse choral
moans, thundering trumpets. Many vowed they'd heard nothing
like it, though a few wrote of its strange familiarity—"a haunting

convergence of forgotten lullabies," wrote a bedazzled reporter. One woman, later revealed to be color-blind, claimed to have heard nothing at all, and was stunned to see those around her so transfixed. No two people seemed to have heard the same piece.

What are we to make of such an event? Lamark's notebooks from this period speak of something called the "harmonoscope," a machine designed to convert harmonic frequencies into specific hues, though neither the device nor the plans for such a thing were ever recovered.

The chief debate that arose during Lamark's brief reemergence in the 1920s was whether *Chromatica* was a work of proto-cinema or of post-tonal music. A case could have been made for both, or just as easily, neither. The Dada movement lauded the Illusionists for their embrace of the ill-defined and abstruse, as well as their disregard for artistic institutions—indeed, Lamark had never considered himself an artist or composer at all, merely an inventor with an interest in chimerical effect. What congealed from the controversy was that as Lamark's genius was not limited to performance, his works should not be canonized in any one school of thought or artistic tradition. Their incompleteness, their transience, were as crucial to their being understood as language was to speech. Tristan Tzara, the grand dragon of Dada, believed they were best held as demonstrations of possibility, rather than imperishable monuments to established values or truths: to memorialize them was to distort their very intention.

From the distance of forty years—in gay, prewar Paris—these may have seemed like pressing concerns, but at the time there were far graver matters. At the forefront, there was the grisly conflict that flared when news of an epileptic child who'd attended the exhibition and asphyxiated as a result of an unaided seizure made the front page of *La Fraternité*. The audience, apparently hypnotized by Lamark's spectacle, had failed to notice the convulsions and suffocated whimpers of the nine-year-old boy, and he died tragically the following evening.

To the Christians who believed Lamark possessed of wicked spirits, this confirmed their suspicions: he was the devil on Earth, conjuring infernal visions and sacrificing children. That same night, a throng of wrathful zealots proceeded to picket Elysium Laboratories. They marched through the cobblestone streets, carrying torches and chanting oaths of vengeance. They shattered the theater's windows, overturned the seats and smashed everything in sight.

The community was unsympathetic to Lamark's loss. The inventor-dramatist was blacklisted from every institution in town—there was no lawyer, insurance agent or bank that would stand behind him. Shortly thereafter, what was left of Elysium was barricaded shut, and Lamark embarked on a journey back north, never to return.

VIII

When Lamark died in 1884, the year international time zones were standardized, his estate lawyer happened upon the aged, cherry wood cabinet he'd inherited from his father two decades prior. In it were dozens of ledgers, diaries, sketchpads, scrapbooks, blueprints and other documents Lamark had compiled over the years. Many contained private opinions regarding his contemporaries, from the opera of Wagner ("[t]he only name worth mentioning in the history of the medium") to the violin concerti of Paganini ("insufferable Italian rubbish"), as well as endless ruminations on politics and religion.

The mechanical journals were released to the Technology Institute where they were studied by Professor Jameson Boggs, an early admirer. Boggs claimed to have recovered dozens of ingenious designs—a variable speed player piano, a keyboard with forty tones to the octave, hydraulic percussion instruments capable of producing thunderous tones.

Toward the very end, Lamark's notes grew more ambitious still. He described a "neo-Pythagorean" theory of celestial harmony—the ancient belief that planets emitted pitches equivalent to the overtone series—and included plans for a machine to record the frequencies of tectonic plates underfoot. Lamark was also convinced that the body itself contained a "row of equal-tempered sonorities far beyond the threshold of the human ear" and sketched many ideas on how to amplify them before turning his attentions elsewhere.

Perhaps his greatest unfinished project was the *Temple of Music*. Based on Robert Fludd's illustration, itself an extrapolation of the blacksmith shop whose clanging anvils had famously inspired Pythagoras to develop his monochord, Lamark drafted extensive architectural plans for a giant enclosed space rich with nested harmonic systems. Columns of air would sift through tiny shafts in the floorboards; pulleys and water weights were networked into sound channels. In certain rooms, one's footfalls would echo and resonate on hollowed stone panels; in others, opening a door would slide a bow across a thin metal beam and sing.

The same year Boggs devoted himself to Lamark's journals, however, a tremendous oil fire raged along the Thames when a tanker crashed into the docks—the result of a drunken captain. Miraculously, no lives were lost, but several canal-facing buildings including the Institute were engulfed in flames. Lamark's legacy was lost forever, save a few punishing reviews and the foot-notes in Samson Peterdi's posthumous memoirs.

This is not to suggest that his spirit—or, if you will, his leg-end—was consumed along with it. As well as having been resur-rected by the Dadaists, albeit tenuously, Lamark's name enjoyed intermittent rehabilitation, even fame. The Russian composer Alexander Scriabin, in a letter to Provofiev, credited *Chromatica* as the inspiration behind his "lighting symphony," *Prometheus*. The magician-composer was also the subject of H. P. Lovecraft's early horror story, "Sleight of Hand." As late as the 1970s, the Hungarian Illusionist Society included Lamark in their annual séance, along with Robert-Houdin and Alexander Herrmann. But, regrettably, the name Phelix Lamark is nowadays scarcely mentioned in or out of the academy.

What is one to say of his absence? Indeed, the world has again repaginated, inexorably—recomposed itself to fit another age, one in which there appears little place for grey areas, elliptical paths or blurred boundaries. What use have we for the recon-dite and enigmatic in a globalized, iron-fist marketplace? Was Lamark's premonition correct? Have we hyper-specialized past the point where it benefits us?

One hopes that things are not so irreversible, that his spirit will be rejuvenated in some small way, perhaps through a new crop of curious minds who will vivify our forgotten love of in-betweens, could-bes and not-just-yets.

Robert Fludd, *De Systemate Musico* (1617). Goethe described architecture as "frozen music." Lamark sought to realize this metaphor.

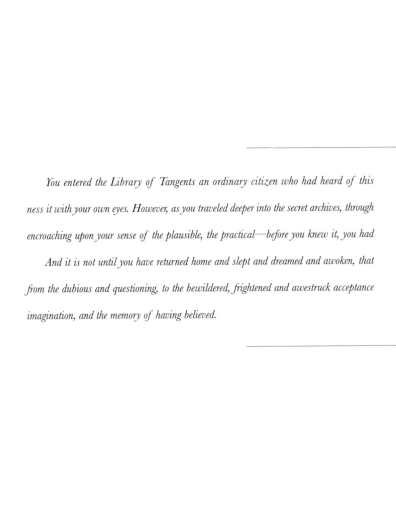

You entered the Library of Tangents an ordinary citizen who had heard of this

ness it with your own eyes. However, as you traveled deeper into the secret archives, through

encroaching upon your sense of the plausible, the practical—before you knew it, you had

And it is not until you have returned home and slept and dreamed and awoken, that

from the dubious and questioning, to the bewildered, frightened and awestruck acceptance

imagination, and the memory of having believed.

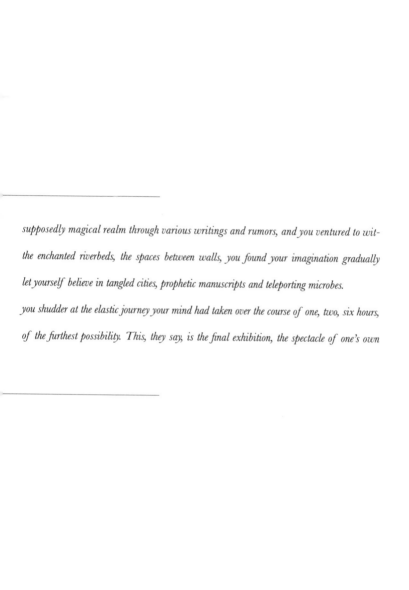

supposedly magical realm through various writings and rumors, and you ventured to wit-

the enchanted riverbeds, the spaces between walls, you found your imagination gradually

let yourself believe in tangled cities, prophetic manuscripts and teleporting microbes.

you shudder at the elastic journey your mind had taken over the course of one, two, six hours,

of the furthest possibility. This, they say, is the final exhibition, the spectacle of one's own

ALEX ROSE has published stories and essays for the *Reading Room*, the *North American Review*, the *Providence Journal*, the *Forward*, *DIAGRAM* and others. His hypertext novel, *Synapse: The Weblog of Catherine Bloom*, was serialized in the Hotel St. George Press Arts Quarterly during the winter of 2007 (www.hsgpress.com/laboratory/).

He has also directed many award-winning short films and animations, which have appeared on Comedy Central, Show-Time and the BBC, as well as in over two dozen festivals worldwide.

He currently resides in Brooklyn, New York.

This book is the second release from

HOTEL ST. GEORGE PRESS

Please visit us online.

OUR WEBSITE, a literary and arts quarterly, is host to a wide assortment of media—strange films, dubious histories, sonic ephemera and other curious works of fiction and fancy.

www.hsgpress.com

HOTEL ST. GEORGE PRESS is an independently curated imprint of Akashic Books. Our titles are available at bookstores, on our website, and are distributed to the trade by Consortium.